BLOOD

HARVEST

RUSTY SHOOP

PublishAmerica
Baltimore

First printing

All characters in this book are fictitious, and any resemblance to real persons, living or dead, is coincidental.

PublishAmerica has allowed this work to remain exactly as the author intended, verbatim, without editorial input.

ISBN: 1-60474-478-2
PUBLISHED BY PUBLISHAMERICA, LLLP
www.publishamerica.com
Baltimore

Printed in the United States of America

Dedicated to my lovely wife Diane and my step-daughter Debby whose encouragement and enthusiasm were instrumental in getting *Blood Harvest* into print.

CHAPTER 1

Pop, pop, pop. Three shots from a .22 caliber Beretta rang out in the cold San Jacinto Valley night. A Hispanic man in his mid-thirties knelt in the dirt with his hands cuffed behind him. As the .22 slugs slammed into the back of his head, he lurched forward, falling with a muffled thud, face first, into the soft soil of the fallow cotton field. Standing in stone cold silence, three men stood over the body as a pool of blood quickly formed around the victim's head and the body finished its final spasms of life. Even though several farm houses were within easy earshot of the gunfire on a normal night, all three of the trench coat covered figures knew that on this night the thick valley fog would easily gobble up any sound made by the most vocal of firearms.

For a few brief seconds, the three stoic figures stared at their work as a painter might stand back and gaze at what he had just put down on canvas. The shooter slid the Beretta back into the deep pocket of the full length London Fog, another retrieved the stainless steel handcuffs. The three men then climbed inside a large sedan and drove away, leaving only the dead Mexican, three shell casings, and three sets of cowboy boot prints behind.

CHAPTER 2

Jake Adams stood in one corner of the newsroom reading over the scripts that would soon become Eyewitness News at Six. To the casual observer it might look like Jake was moving in slow motion compared to what was going on around him. And what was going on around him was the usual helter-skelter scene that always plagued the newsroom at 5:45, with a live broadcast only fifteen minutes away. But Jake had been in the news business in Butterfield for a long time, and he paid no attention to the madness as he slowly strolled toward the news set, head down, reading over his scripts.

Jake was accustomed to the chaos. Every newscast came down to the last few minutes. Tape editors and photographers scurrying around like mice in a maze with newly edited video in their hands...producers screaming at reporters that their scripts weren't finished or their supers weren't in the computer yet. At ten till five the public address system came alive with a crackle followed by the deep voice of the show's director, Hack Davis, serenely telling everyone involved in the upcoming broadcast (in his best fasten-your-seat-belts pilot's voice) that the show would soon begin, with or without them. Hack was like a god as far as the broadcast was concerned. Once the red light came on he told everyone including Jake what to do and when to do it. And the robust bearded man handled every broadcast with not an ounce of ego, but with a supreme sense that, and Hack loved to use this cliche', "the show must go on."

Jake and Hack were always on the same page. People in the newsroom called them the News Brothers, because when the teleprompter started to roll they both knew one thing…they were going to put on the best news hour in town. Even with pieces of the on-air puzzle falling into place at the last minute like little news meteors from the sky, this show would be like Eyewitness News broadcasts every night, it would be very good.

Jake Adams was an old-timer in the news business in Butterfield. He'd been handing the local residents a capsule of their world in video and sound bites since the early '70s. At nearly sixty, the years had treated Jake well. He was nearly six feet tall with silver-gray hair and moustache. People said he looked a lot like Paul Newman in *The Color of Money*, although Jake imagined his looks, and his sense of humor, a lot more like Johnny Carson. The golf course was about the only place Jake got anything resembling exercise. A hearty dose of God-given energy and metabolism kept most of the weight off. His trademark voice reflected years of hard drinking and smoking, both of which were now just bad memories, although Jake did enjoy a cold beer every now and then at a local hangout called The Dog House. Jake would have moved on to a larger market years ago, but he found life in the slow lane in San Jacinto County, in the Central Valley of California, much to his liking.

Jake was a simple man, and he loved the simple pleasures that the Butterfield area offered. It was just a couple of hours to the coast and lots of sand surf and sunshine. It was just an hour or so to the Sierra Nevada Mountains where his Jeep Wrangler could take him to a secluded location where the sounds of the city gave way to the chirping of birds and the occasional howl of a coyote…and where the often acrid exhaust filled air of the valley was replaced by the crisp clean smell of pine.

Jake had all the time he needed to spend on his excursions out of town. He'd been divorced for nearly twenty years. Jake, once a hot-shot reporter in southern California, had responded to an ad in a trade journal about the on-air job in Butterfield. He got the job and he and his wife had moved to Butterfield. Jake loved the small town. His wife did not. She longed for the hustle and bustle of Southern California where they'd met. One day she announced she was returning to the 'rat race' as Jake called it. Jake decided to stay on in Butterfield. The rest, as they say, is history.

Butterfield itself was a city of no more than a few hundred thousand people even if the census took you all the way to the San Jacinto County line. Even with television markets like San Francisco to the north and Los Angeles to the south beckoning at various junctures in his career, Jake felt at home in Butterfield, and after twenty-five years on the air Jake figured he would retire, maybe even die here.

Of course everyone in Butterfield knew Jake. He couldn't go anywhere in public without somebody recognizing him and wanting to talk. But for the most part Jake didn't mind. He loved people. And being from the old school of reporting he knew that any good conversation could turn into a great story idea.

It was five minutes until show time when Jake settled into his chair behind the anchor desk next to his female co-anchor.

He said a quick hello to the two young studio camera operators who were busy lining up their shots and getting some last minute instructions over their headsets from Hack. The last few scripts were given a quick once-over and Jake was ready for the broadcast to begin.

After years of being in the business, every hour-long news show sounded eerily similar to other six o'clock shows. Today three people died in a car crash out on the interstate, and as usual a big-rig was involved. One house burned to the ground. Everyone got out safely thanks to the warning of one of the family's children, who, Butterfield Fire Department investigators now say, may have actually started the fire by testing the pyrotechnic properties of an entire box of wooden matches. And a couple of City Parks employees were under investigation for allegedly helping to set up other city employees with prostitutes in a park near the city's red light district. Except for the faces and the places, as Jake would say, the news around Butterfield was pretty predictable and hardly ever earth shaking.

When the end of Eyewitness News at Six finally rolled up on the white on black teleprompter the only thing that remained was the "kicker" as it was called in the business. Most often the *kicker* was read by Jake's female co-anchor, Lisa Kraft, a beautiful young olive skinned woman of exceptional talent. Jake knew Lisa would only be in Butterfield a few years before she would move on to a larger market and Jake would be faced with breaking in another co-anchor. Such was the peril of being the perennial on-air pundit in Butterfield. The "kicker" story was usually an offering from the animal kingdom with a happy ending designed to let the audience forget for a moment all the death and destruction from around the world that had dominated the news for the last hour. The kicker however, was often the target of Jake's rather bizarre sense of humor. The behind the scenes crew loved to wait and see if Jake was going to skewer the players in the show's finale', as would many of the folks at home. Tonight Jake would not disappoint.

Lisa Kraft launched into a lovely little tale about a beached baby whale along the Northern California Coast that was finally coaxed back into the ocean by a number of bearded friends of the Earth with PhD's. As the video of the happy whale family quickly faded back to the set, Jake, in a very monotone voice turned to Lisa and said, "That's too bad in a way, that Monterey Bay baby whale jerky is some of the best around." Jake turned emotionless to the camera and said a sincere "goodnight everybody." Lisa Kraft turned to the camera and said a polite "goodnight" in a tone that wreaked of "don't mind Jake, he can't help it." The studio lights went dim, and the network news came up in living rooms all over Butterfield.

As Jake walked off the set, wondering if the phones would light up with the calls from irate whale lovers, he heard the police scanner screeching to life in the background. A Sheriff's Department dispatcher was calling for a patrol car to roll on a possible homicide. And by the static filled conversation Jake heard filling the airwaves, another body had been found in a field southwest of town.

CHAPTER 3

The fields of San Jacinto County were home to a variety of crops. Cotton was king, and immediately after harvest in the early Fall, the cotton fields were plowed under to prevent boll weevil infestation. The fields then sat idle during the winter unless the farmer decided to plant a crop of winter wheat to be turned into hay for the local dairy industry. The field that was now drawing the attention of the Sheriff's Department and the Eyewitness Newsroom was empty, except for a young couple in a pickup truck who were apparently in search of a secluded place away from their parents. It was these teenagers who came across the gruesome sight of a bloated and fly infested corpse.

Dead bodies were nothing new in Butterfield. The city did have its share of murders. Domestic disputes and barroom brawls took a modest toll on the population. And for several years now, gangs from Los Angeles and San Francisco had found their way to Butterfield. Out of town gang-bangers figured that the city limit sign that said "Butterfield" might as well have read "Bumpkinville." But the law in Butterfield was a bit different than in the big cities. The local Sheriff's

Department didn't see a lot of violent crime, but when they did, they figured a shoot-first, ask questions later philosophy would be the best way to keep the violence to a minimum. So now the word was out, and the bad guys knew, that if you held up a liquor store or robbed a bank in Butterfield, you would likely wind up in a shootout with the law, and your surviving relatives would soon be going to your funeral.

Still, small numbers of gang members crept in, but as long as the drug dealing and the drive-byes stayed in East Butterfield, the local cops were content with letting the town's gang members kill themselves off. Oh sure, the badges would head over to the east side of town when a shooting occurred. But since no witnesses wanted to talk anyway, fearing for their own lives, murder in East Butterfield was pretty much just a matter of paperwork. And for the local media, a shooting on the eastside was a story, but usually one that ended with the line, "Sheriff's investigators have no leads, and no suspects."

But what was going out over the scanner now was being monitored very closely, and an Eyewitness News crew was headed to the scene as fast as the Sheriff's Department. The news crew knew the back roads as well as any deputy, and it was a forgone conclusion that the newsroom would soon have some great video of a corpse that they would never be able to show to the viewing public, along with sound bites from a couple of young people who were scared out of their wits by their grisly discovery.

Chrissy Carr was the eleven o'clock producer on the Assignment Desk when the Sheriff's Dispatcher called for a patrol car to head out to the field southwest of town. As the young producer continued to listen to the scanner, she turned to Jake and off-handedly remarked, "too bad the body wasn't found a half hour earlier."

Jake tossed back a quick nod and a half grin, knowing exactly what Chrissy meant. It was those primal journalistic instincts telling the young producer what a great "breaking story" the body would have been during the Six O'clock show, and how reporting the disgusting discovery live on the air, even without video, would have made the Eyewitness News team look like the big dog that it was. Even though no one in the newsroom prayed for death and destruction, if bad stuff was going to happen anyway, everyone who worked in the Eyewitness Newsroom wanted to get the story first.

Now, seeing that Chrissy had the situation under control, Jake decided to take his dinner break. And when he got back, she could fill him in on the details of the decomposing body.

Dinner for Jake usually consisted of sitting down at one of four local eateries. All were local Mom and Pop operations. Two were diners. One was Mexican, the other Italian. Jake never went home for dinner. He rarely went home for anything except to sleep and change clothes. Even though he'd been divorced for a long time, Jake still owned their modest home in one of the older neighborhoods near downtown Butterfield where the Eyewitness News studios were located. But it was now just a big lonely house…a place to hang his clothes…and sleep. Friends often suggested that he either sell the house and move into something cozier, or get a dog. Jake didn't want to sell the house, too much hassle was the excuse, and he didn't want a dog, for the same reason.

Jake chose Lurene's Diner. It was close to work, and the menu was simple. He didn't feel like making a lot of decisions tonight. And since it was Wednesday, Jake knew what he was having anyway. Wednesday was meat loaf and mashed potatoes night. Jake would tell the waitress to put the green peas in a side dish so he could smother the meat and potatoes with ketchup.

The fog was getting thick as Jake drove the short distance to the diner. Winter in the Valley was often foggy, sometimes for days or even weeks at a time, and people who lived in the valley would joke that they forgot what the sun looked like. If Carl Sandburg's fog came in on little cat feet, then the valley fog rolled in like "The Blob", consuming everything in its path. This batch of Tule fog had settled in just a few days ago after the last front moved through and left just enough rain behind to make the pea soup especially murky.

Up ahead the neon "Lurene's" sign stood out like a friendly beacon in the mist. Jake pulled into the parking lot, climbed out of his Jeep, and headed for the double glass doors of the diner. As he entered, Jake paused for a moment to let the warm smells of the diner wash over him. The aromatic ambience included homemade chili and soup simmering in the kitchen…along with meatloaf, hand crafted biscuits, and of course, Lurene's famous apple pie. They all hit you as soon as you entered the doorway, and even if you weren't hungry when you walked in, your appetite was quickly kicked into high gear. Jake headed to the back where a blue vinyl corner booth awaited.

Millie, the waitress, had already seen the red Jeep pulling into the parking lot, and as Jake slid into the booth, Millie met him there.

"How you doin' tonight, Jake?" the pretty blond waitress asked.

"Cold," Jake replied…"If there's anything that would make me move out of Butterfield it's this depressing fog."

Millie had a menu under her arm, but instead of handing it to Jake she simply asked, "the usual?"

"What else?,"replied Jake with a friendly smile.

"Peas on the side?," Millie asked, knowing the answer.

Jake's smile broadened, "am I that predictable?"

"Only when it comes to green peas. I'll bring the truckload of ketchup."

Millie was Lurene's granddaughter. Lurene died about ten years ago, but Lurene's son Ben and his wife, Dolores had opted to keep the popular diner in the family instead of selling it to a McFranchise. Millie, Ben and Dolores' daughter, was going to the local junior college, and worked evenings at the diner. She was a beautiful young girl, and very flirtatious, especially with Jake. But she wasn't serious. Millie had waitressed long enough to know that brightening the day of a customer meant more money in tips.

A few moments later, as Jake sat staring out through the large window at the haze covered traffic lights, a huge plate of meat loaf and mashed potatoes arrived.

"Here you go Jake...and a nice fat bottle of Heinz. You look a little preoccupied tonight. Rough day?"

"No," said Jake..."a late breaker. Another body found in a field outside of town."

"Like the other ones?," Millie asked as she busied herself cleaning up the mess on the table next to Jake.

"Don't know yet. Sure sounds familiar. It's been over a month though...we should know more when I get back to work."

"Too many bodies in Butterfield if you ask me," said Millie as she carried a tray full of dirty dishes toward the kitchen.

This was the fifth body found in a local field in as many months. The other four were shot in the back of the head with a small caliber weapon. Two were Hispanic. Two were African-American. There had been no arrests, and according to the Sheriff's Department, no solid leads. The only information the news department could get was that they had all been shot at the scene, not killed somewhere else and dumped, and all the locations were similar...various fields just outside of town.

Jake took his last bite of meat loaf, washed it down with coffee, and decided to head back to work.

"See you later Millie," Jake called into the kitchen. "Better get back and find out who the dead guy is."

Millie quickly came out and gave Jake a smile to help keep him warm out in the fog…"I'll let you tell me all about it on the t-v tonight. See you soon." Millie's eyes followed the silver haired anchorman as he left the diner, climbed into his Jeep, and disappeared into the fog.

Moments later Jake pulled into the Eyewitness News parking lot. He climbed out of the Jeep, braced himself against the chill, and with key in hand he headed for the security door that led to the newsroom. The valley fog could cut right through a person, and Jake's body gave a shudder of pleasure as it met the warmth inside the building.

Chrissy Carr tapped away at her keyboard and never even looked up from the computer as Jake headed for the producer's desk. It was as quiet as a tomb in the newsroom now. Jake loved the nightshift. All the execs had gone home, and the only people in the entire, mostly darkened building, were the skeleton crew putting together the eleven o'clock broadcast. Jake leaned against the elevated countertop where the producers and the assignment editor sat. Still, Chrissy stared at her computer screen.

"So," said Jake. "What's with the body?"

Chrissy was absorbed in the script she was writing, and as Jake's words jogged her brain she shifted into another gear.

"Oh, yeah. Not much to tell. Same as the other four. Three small caliber bullets in the back of the head. Shot right there…execution style. Been there for a couple of days by the looks of the body." Chrissy looked up from her computer. "What do you think's going on with these bodies Jake, connected or coincidence?"

"Don't know," replied Jake. "Isn't the Sheriff's Department saying anything else?"

"Oh sure" said Chrissy sarcastically. "It's in your eleven o'clock script. No leads, no suspects. The usual."

"Body got a name?" asked Jake.

"That's in the script too"…Chrissy followed her index finger through the scribbles on her note pad…"Rudolph Juarez Sandoval…34 year old Hispanic male."

Jake wandered over to his desk to start going through the eleven o'clock show. As he logged on to his computer, the chirp of the telephone broke the silence in the newsroom. "I got it," Jake said as he picked up the receiver. "Eyewitness Newsroom," Jake said politely.

A woman with a Hispanic accent was on the other end of the phone. "Is this the news people?" she asked.

"Yes it is," Jake replied.

The Mexican woman's voice sounded shy…"Is Jake Adams there?"

"This is Jake…can I help you?"

"My name is Maria." Her voice sounded like she'd been crying…and all at once the words came pouring out of the Hispanic woman's mouth with a sense of urgency. "My husband's name is Rudy Sandoval…the deputy just came here and said they found Rudy's body in a field. I need to talk to you right away. It's about Rudy…and the other four men who were killed."

Jake suddenly realized he had Rudolph Juarez Sandoval's widow on the phone…and she sounded scared.

CHAPTER 4

Eyewitness News at Eleven, with its lead story of the body of Rudolph Juarez Sandoval, was over, and Jake wasted no time. He said a hasty goodnight to the crew, climbed into his Jeep, and headed for east Butterfield. Why did Maria Sandoval sound so frightened on the phone? What did she know about the other four dead men? And how did it all tie in with her own husband's murder? Jake didn't have a clue. The only thing he did know for sure was that according to the address that Maria Sandoval had given him over the phone, Jake was about to drive right into the heart of gang territory.

The fog was thick. Visibility was probably down to a hundred feet or less. The light from lonely street lamps and traffic signals gave off a ghostly glow as Jake headed toward Jefferson Avenue. At Jefferson Jake took a left and headed east. Jefferson Avenue was a paradox. As it passed through downtown, it was home to some of the city's most prominent tributes to justice and freedom...City Hall...The Sheriff's Department...County Council Chambers...and the County

Courthouse. But a mile and a half to the east, Jefferson Avenue passed through the heart of one of the most notorious parts of town. Gang territory. And that's where Jake Adams was headed.

As he crossed Brand Boulevard into east Butterfield, Jake was suddenly thankful for the fog. It gave him a shield of sorts…a Star Trek type cloaking device that would hopefully make him invisible to whatever peril might be out there in the east Butterfield night. But whatever fears Jake might have entertained, they were far outweighed by his journalistic curiosity, as he wondered what Maria Sandoval knew about five murders.

Jake's hastily transcribed map showed he was quickly coming up on his first turn. He took a right on Citrus Street…followed that for a couple of blocks until he came to Orchard Court…and took a left. Jake found himself on a short cul-de-sac with just a few porch lights burning, and 1931 Orchard Court was not one of them. A dim glow from somewhere in the house was the only light visible as Jake approached his destination at the end of the street. The Red Wrangler rolled to a stop. Jake turned the engine off and rolled down his window. The sound of a dog barking somewhere in the distance was the only thing Jake heard, except for the pounding of his own heart. He sat and stared at the house, debating his next move. His decision was soon made for him. A darkened figure, silhouetted by the faint light inside the house, appeared at the front door, and with a wave of a hand motioned for Jake to come inside. Jake stepped out of the Jeep and headed towards the house. A strange sensation overtook Jake as he took his first few steps. He suddenly felt he was in an old black and white Bogart movie as he made his way through the veil of fog to this midnight rendezvous with a stranger he'd only met on the phone a short time ago. As he drew closer to the porch, Jake saw the figure of a woman standing in the open doorway. As Jake approached she silently turned and entered the house. Jake followed, closing the door behind him.

The smell of cigarette smoke filled Jake's nostrils as he followed Maria Sandoval down a darkened hallway toward the only light in the house. At the end of the hallway Jake found himself in a small but neat kitchen with a small butcher-block table surrounded by four wooden stools. On the table was a half empty pack of Marlboros…and a full ashtray.

Maria Sandoval immediately reached for the pack of cigarettes and shook one out. She tapped the filter end twice on the table…grabbed a nearby pack of matches and lit the Marlboro, tossing the match in among the other ashes and cigarette butts. She took a long drag from the cigarette and inhaled deeply. Maria was a tall woman…about five foot eight or nine, with long dark hair. Her small brown eyes were set into a thin weathered face that reflected years of hard living. She wore a gray hooded sweatshirt and jeans. But even with her rough outer facade…Jake guessed Maria was only in her mid thirties.

She pulled one of the stools closer to the table and sat down. "Please, sit down Mister Adams." Maria spoke in a thick Mexican accent. It was a deep raspy voice…probably the result of years of serious chain smoking.

Jake followed her lead and took a seat. Maria Sandoval had yet to make eye contact with Jake…and the silence in the house…in the middle of the night…in the dense fog…was deafening.

"I'm sorry about your husband." Jake wanted to break the ice, but the words echoed hollow and insincere in his head. He decided silence was his next best choice. He waited for Maria to speak.

Maria's eyes were fixed on the only decoration in the kitchen, a picture on the wall of the Virgin Mary holding the Christ Child. Her eyes never left the picture as she began to speak. "I will tell you what I know. After we bury Rudy...I will leave town."

Jake remained silent. He sensed that Rudolph Sandoval's widow was about to give him the information that had lured him deep into gang territory on a foggy night.

She did.

Maria turned her eyes from the picture on the wall...she crushed out her cigarette in the ashtray, and turned to look at Jake. "My husband was a drug dealer...the other four men who were killed were drug dealers too."

The comment was so frank...so matter of fact that it took Jake by surprise. Everyone in the Eyewitness Newsroom thought the murders were related somehow...now the widow of Rudolph Sandoval had tied them together.

Maria continued. "Rudy knew the other men...not that well...but they knew each other"...She grabbed the pack of Marlboro's again..."After the first two were murdered Rudy and me we started to worry." Maria tapped the filter of the unlit cigarette on the table. She grabbed the pack of matches, scratched one on the rough surface and lit the cigarette, again inhaling deeply. Maria was now refocused on the Madonna. "After the last two were found dead, we talked about leaving town...but the money...it's hard to give up." Maria paused for a moment. She turned slowly to look at Jake. Tears started to fill her eyes. "They killed Rudy Mister Adams...the same people who killed the others killed my Rudy."

Jake figured it was time to wade in with a few questions...time to let the journalistic juices take over. "How do you know that...who do you think killed your husband... and the others?"

"I'm not sure." Maria tried to compose herself. "But this is crazy. They all sold dope…and they're all dead…my Rudy's gone…and I'm scared Mister Adams." Maria crushed out her half smoked cigarette in the ashtray. She brushed her long dark hair back with both hands and let out a huge sigh of frustration as she turned again to look at the picture of the Madonna.

"Mrs. Sandoval, I can't begin to imagine how you must feel…but please let me ask you…why did you call me?"

Maria slowly turned her head to look at Jake again…as her eyes caught his, she slowly started to shake her head. "I'm not real sure…I didn't know anybody else to call…and I had to say something to somebody. I see you on the news every night…and it just seems like I can trust you…I…I don't know what else to say."

"You can trust me, Maria." Jake tried to reassure the grieving woman that her invitation wasn't in vain…"I'm just not sure exactly what I can do for you."

"Maybe nothing…maybe you can find out who killed Rudy. I can't stay here. Five people are dead…for all I know…I may be next."

"Mrs. Sandoval," Jake asked. "Do you think a rival drug dealer killed your husband and the other men? Did your husband have any enemies that you know of?"

"I don't know" she replied. "People do crazy things on drugs. I wish we'd never gotten into this. All these drugs…it's the devil's work. And now we're paying the price."

"I understand you're fear…and I promise you…I'll at least ask some questions…I can't promise you anything…but I'll see what I can find out." Jake was at a loss as to what else to say to this woman who just lost her husband and now feared for her own life. Jake felt sorry for Maria, even if her husband was a drug dealer. He wasn't sure what he could find out. He just didn't want to tell her there was nothing he could do.

The small kitchen became silent. Finally, Jake said the only thing he could think of. "Mrs. Sandoval, I promise…I'll do what I can." Jake got up from the stool and looked down on Maria's tear stained face. "I promise. Good night Mrs. Sandoval."

Maria Sandoval tried to muster a "thank you" grin. Jake turned and walked down the darkened hallway and out the front door into the dense fog. He climbed in his Jeep, started the engine and headed out of the cul-de-sac. It was still so foggy that the streetlight at the end of the block was barely visible. So foggy in fact, that Jake would never have noticed or heard the other car that had entered the cul-de-sac within the short time he had been in Maria Sandoval's house. The occupant of that car was now lying out of sight on the front seat as Jake drove by…but he would soon get out of the car…to pay his own visit to Maria Sandoval

CHAPTER 5

Sleep eluded Jake most of the night. His midnight conversation with Maria Sandoval combined with the image of a body lying in a field wouldn't leave Jake's thoughts. Even when the sandman finally succeeded in knocking Jake out for the night, the past evening's events dominated his subconscious. In a dream Jake was standing in an empty field. The earthy smell of freshly plowed dirt filled his nostrils. The frigid fog wrapped him in an icy bear hug. Suddenly the hazy glow of headlights appeared. A figure was dragged out of the back seat and around to the front of the car. The shadow-man dropped to his knees, silhouetted by the headlights. From the side, as if making some sort of surreal off-stage entrance, another darkened figure appeared. The glint of a nickel-plated handgun came into view. Three shots rang out…muffled like a pillow by the fog. The kneeling figure fell face first into the dirt. Slowly, the shooter turned to face Jake. But just as his face was about to become visible, Jake awoke.

The open-beamed ceiling of his bedroom was the first thing that met Jake's eyes. Sweat covered Jake's body and soaked the sheets beneath him. His heart pounded. His chest rose and fell with each heavy breath.

Jake's gradual return to consciousness revealed just what a fitful night it had been. The sheets were half pulled off the bed, the blanket was on the floor, Jake's head was at the foot of the bed.

"It was just a dream," Jake thought to himself. But what had brought on the dream was very real. His late night conversation with Maria Sandoval had made one thing crystal clear. If Maria Sandoval was right, five men had been executed because they were drug dealers…but by whom…and why.

Forcing himself to get up, Jake rolled over and sat on the edge of the bed. The faded jeans were still on the floor where he'd tossed them the night before. He tugged them on and groggily headed down the hallway, tapping the thermostat on the wall to the "ON" position as he passed. The tile floor of the kitchen was cold against the bottoms of his feet as he made his way to the dishwasher. He grabbed a clean coffee cup from the top rack and filled it with tap water. He opened the nearby microwave oven door, set the cup inside and punched the number two on the digital pad. To complete his morning ritual, Jake headed out through the living room to the front door to pick up the morning paper from the driveway. The fog grabbed him like a blanket of ice. Barefoot and shirtless he raced for the paper, which was in the driveway. Luckily it was wrapped in a plastic bag or it would have been soaked by the ubiquitous dew.

The microwave timer still showed a minute fifteen seconds when Jake returned to the kitchen. He pulled the rubber band and the plastic wrapper from the paper, tossed them aside, and unfolded the paper. Opening the cabinet above his head, Jake retrieved a jar of instant coffee crystals. The seconds on the microwave counted down under Jake's close supervision. He hated the sound the microwave made when it was done. As the digital clock showed 30 seconds, the whir of the central heating system kicked into gear and Jake felt warmed just by the sound. Finally the seconds on the microwave worked their way backwards to five. Before they hit zero, Jake tapped the latch on the microwave door just in time to stop the small oven from making its irritating buzzing sound. Jake twisted the top off the coffee crystal jar, reached for a spoon from the drawer, and added a heaping amount of dark brown granules to the hot water. Jake stirred the dark brew vigorously as he savored the first smell of coffee drifting up to his nostrils. As he lifted the steaming brew to his lips, Jake turned his eyes to the opened paper on the tile countertop. He almost choked on his coffee as the headline screamed out at him, doing more on this foggy morning than the instant coffee ever would. "WIDOW OF MURDER VICTIM COMMITS SUICIDE."

On the front page of the Butterfield Californian was a large photo of the charred remains of 1931 Orchard Court, the home of Maria Sandoval, the same house that Jake had visited only hours before. According to the fire department the blaze broke out about one in the morning. Jake had left at around 12:30. According to the article, Maria Sandoval had been found in the living room. Suicide was suspected because arson was definitely the cause. A gasoline can had been found near the body. According the quote from Sheriff's Detective Al Copolo, it was believed that Mrs. Sandoval was depressed over the death of her husband and set the house on fire, taking her own life in the process. The article went on to say that earlier in the evening a Sheriff's Deputy had gone to the Sandoval home to deliver the news about her husband's death. And investigators believe that is what triggered Mrs. Sandoval's torching of her own home, and herself.

Jake was in shock as he turned his attention back to the front-page photo. Maria Sandoval certainly didn't seem suicidal the night before. But she did say that she had to leave. Could suicide be what she meant? But if all five murders were tied together, and Jake believed they were, could Maria have been the sixth? But why would someone kill her? And at the moment, possibly the most important question of all, at least to Jake, if someone did murder Maria Sandoval, did they see Jake leaving her house just after midnight?

Too many questions, not enough answers. Maybe the paper was right. Maybe it was a suicide. Maybe Jake was just too caught up in his own paranoia. One thing Jake knew for sure, this was not the time to circle the wagons. If what Maria Sandoval said was true, it was time for Jake to start asking some questions and getting some answers. And if Maria Sandoval's death wasn't suicide, Jake's own life may depend on the answers he came up with.

Jake left the paper lying open on the kitchen counter, and taking a large gulp of black coffee he headed down the hall to the shower, to get ready for a full day of investigative reporting.

CHAPTER 6

After showering and shaving, Jake grabbed a clean white dress shirt from the closet and a clean pair of Wrangler jeans from a dresser drawer. Jake always wore jeans to work for one very simple reason. They were comfortable. Jake hated suit pants. He thought any wool blend fabric was about the most unnatural thing a person could wear. Even on those occasions where he was expected to dress like a respectable news anchor, Jake opted for the type of all-cotton slacks made by Docker or Hagger. The loneliest job in the world was to be a pair of pants that went to a suit owned by Jake Adams. You hung there in the closet your whole life collecting dust. And anyway, Jake thought, the television camera only sees you from the waist up. Jake grabbed his favorite pair of black cowboy boots from the floor near the foot of the bed, tugged them on, grabbed a multi-colored Jerry Garcia necktie from his tie-rack, a navy blue double-breasted blazer from the closet, and he was ready to head to the station.

The weather was trying to put a positive spin on the events of the past half-day as Jake walked out the front door. The sun was actually trying to break through the thick valley fog. The fog was something even the most knowledgeable of weathermen couldn't figure out. Some days the fog won, some days the sun was victorious. At present, the sun was putting on a great show of force.

The digital clock in the Jeep showed 10:05 as Jake pulled into the Eyewitness News parking lot. He usually didn't show up to work until two or three in the afternoon, so everyone would wonder why he was so early. Jake would just have to say he had a few things to catch up on. He certainly wasn't ready to confide in anyone at work about the things he knew or suspected so far.

Jake unlocked the security door, and walked down the hall to the newsroom, which was fairly quiet at just after ten in the morning. The reporters and photographers would have left for their morning assignments around nine. The dayside assignment editor, David Hasgrove, greeted Jake. "Can I help you sir…you look lost?"

"I must be if I'm here at this hour," Jake responded. "Came in to do a little clean-up work at the old desk. Read about the Sandoval woman in the paper. Anything new?"

"Not much." The short, stout Hasgrove was standing in front of the large assignment board with an erasable felt-tip marker in his hand. All the stories for the day were lined up on the left side of the board. In adjacent columns to the right were the reporter and photographer for the story, the time the story was to be shot, and who was to be contacted along with a phone number. At the very top of the assignment board, in large blue letters was the single word…*Sandoval.* The reporter on the story was Karen Foley. Karen was probably the most experienced reporter in Butterfield. She'd done radio news in town for years before moving on to television. She was especially familiar with the inside workings of local government and law enforcement, and she knew all of the people at the top on a first name basis. She was well liked and well trusted, and that made getting the scoop on many a story that much easier. Karen had seen local officials come and go…some in disgrace. And even when the highest of local officials had gotten in hot water, Karen was always there, microphone and reporter's pad in hand. She'd been around Butterfield for so long that even the biggest of big wigs felt comfortable talking to her. Karen just had a knack of making you feel like family, and that often led to her getting some of the juiciest bits of information about some of the most sensitive topics, and that made Karen Foley an invaluable asset to the Eyewitness News team. In fact, Jake was hoping that Karen had found out something, anything, that would corroborate, or disprove, what Maria Sandoval had told him last night.

Jake sat down at his desk and grabbed his Rolodex. He thumbed through it until he found the name he was looking for, Mario Franklin. Mario might be able to help Jake find out if the five men who were killed were indeed drug dealers. That was the key piece of information that Jake would need to verify Maria Sandoval's late night testimony.

Jake took the handset out of its cradle, punched nine for an outside line and then the number that was on the Rolodex card. After just a couple of rings, a very pleasant African American voice came on the line. "Eastside Evangelical."

Jake knew the woman behind the voice, although he hadn't made a call to the church in some time. "Hi Lavonda…this is Jake at the T-V station. Is Mario around?"

"Lord Jake, it's good to hear your voice. Mario's out in the field right now. You know how he is. Can't sit in this office too long. There's souls out there need savin'."

Lavonda Goodrich could have been a preacher herself. She was a large Black woman with a heart of gold, who could put a smile on your face with just a few words. She'd raised three kids all by herself, and she'd swear on a stack of Bibles that none of her "yunguns" as she liked to call them, would have amounted to a hill of beans if it hadn't been for Mario Franklin.

Mario himself was a story that could easily be turned into a movie. He was raised by a single parent. Mario's father was a diesel mechanic who often worked nights, and that left Mario on his own a lot. In his early teens Mario had started getting involved with gangs. By the time he was fifteen Mario had been into all sorts of trouble. He had a minor wrap sheet with local law enforcement that included a number of petty thefts and burglaries. But it wasn't long before Mario moved on to more serious stuff like dealing drugs. Mario's father tried to talk some sense into him, but Mario was strong willed and figured he knew it all. Then one summer night, Mario's world dramatically and tragically changed. He and some friends were sitting on the steps outside their East Butterfield home when a low rider Chevy came cruising down the street. When the occupants of the car opened fire, Mario and his friends dove for cover. When the shooting was over, the first thing that Mario realized was that his father hadn't come rushing out of the house to see what happened, so Mario rushed into the house to find out why. He found his father lying on the couch with a single bullet wound to the head.

After the funeral, Mario went to live with an Aunt, who started taking Mario to church every Sunday. On just the third Sunday Mario felt the hand of God on his heart during the sermon. He walked down front at the altar call and gave his life to God. From that moment on, there wasn't a gang member or drug dealer in East Butterfield who was safe from the fire and brimstone of Mario Franklin. In fact, Mario got so good at conveying God's message to those who needed to hear it that he eventually started his own church at the urging of not just a few of the East Butterfield faithful. That was how Eastside Evangelical was born.

Jake was hoping Mario could shed a little light on five dead men and one woman...allegedly involved in the local drug trade. "Lavonda, I need to talk with Mario. When do you expect him back?"

"I never expect him. The only time I'm sure he'll be here is on Sunday morning, but if it's important I can page him. I'd give you his cell phone number, but if he's street preachin' he'll get mad as all getout. Can I tell you a little secret Jake? Mario doesn't call 'em cell phones, he calls 'em *hell* phones."

Lavonda broke out in laughter as Jake chuckled and reassured her, "You're secret is safe with me. It is kind of important though. I'm here at the station. I'll wait. Thanks Lavonda, you're the greatest."

"No," Lavonda sweetly replied, "the Lord's the greatest. You wait right there. Mario won't miss a chance to talk to you."

Putting the phone back in its cradle, Jake returned to his Rolodex. He grabbed the black plastic knob and gave it a twist until the "D's" came rolling by. Jake licked his index finger and moved the cards one at a time until he found the name of Billy Denton.

Billy Denton was somewhere in his mid-20s. He'd wanted to be a cop all his life. As a teenager he even had a police scanner from Radio Shack in his bedroom. By the time he reached high school, he was a regular on the newsroom phone circuit...one of those rare news groupies who'd call every time a story idea popped into his head. Billy was also what some people called slow. He was, in fact, mildly retarded, which is partly why he flunked out of Criminal Justice in junior college. But he loved to feel linked somehow to the news and law enforcement, and sometimes, due to his insatiable appetite for listening to the scanner, Billy would wind up at a crime scene at the same time the Deputies did.

Jake ran into Billy while having a beer at The Dog House a few years back. Billy said it was by accident; Jake thought otherwise. Jake figured an autograph and a quick chat would do the trick, but Billy had other ideas. He launched into a heartbreaking tale about how his parents split up when he was very young because of Billy's disabilities. Dad walked out and Mom got hooked on drugs so badly that Billy was bounced around foster homes for years. At age 13, he landed in the home of a retired cop who spun endless yarns about the crime fighting business. That's how Billy got the bug for law enforcement. Jake sort of adopted Billy that night in the Dog House.

Jake had taken Billy fishing a couple of times up in the mountains in his Jeep. Every time they went fishing Jake thought of the old black and white "Andy Griffith Show." There they'd be, walking toward one of Jake's secluded fishing spots, fishing poles and tackle boxes in tow; Jake at six feet, and next to him, with a bit of a bounce in his step, Billy Denton, at about five foot four, with a rosy round cherub face and a blond crew cut that never went more than two weeks without seeing the barbers scissors. Billy Denton would probably be carded at any liquor store in town until he was forty years old.

Billy knew that Jake thought they looked like Andy and Opie walking toward the small lake. That's why he'd taken it upon himself to learn to whistle the theme song from the opening scene of the show. Jake always knew it was coming, and he always burst out laughing as Billy puckered up and whistled all the way to the fishing hole.

And Jake had been the one to get Billy his current job. Knowing Billy's love of law enforcement, Jake had pulled a few strings and called in a few favors to get Billy on as a clerk at the Sheriff's Department. Jake was proud, Billy was elated. And Jake wasn't exactly sure he should call Billy for a favor that might jeopardize his job. But Billy was always calling anyway, volunteering information that he thought might help Jake with a news story. But in the end, Jake figured this was important enough to ask Billy to check out a couple of things.

"Sheriff's Department," a female voice came on the line.

"May I speak with Billy Denton please," Jake asked.

"May I say who's calling?"

"This is Jake Adams."

"Mister Adams," the serious but polite voice responded. "I think Billy is down in the property room right now. Would you like to leave a message?"

"Well..." Jake was in the process of responding when he was interrupted.

"Speak of the devil...here he comes now. Billy, Jake Adams on line one."

Jake heard a 'thank you' in the background and then the polite voice again. "He'll be here in just a moment. Nice talking with you Mr. Adams."

"Thank you," Jake replied.

The excited and youthful voice that came on the line could have come from a little league baseball player who'd just hit his first home run. "Jake, what's up?"

"Not much buddy, how's it going down at headquarters?"

"Great Jake. I was just down in the property room, giving some serial numbers to Sergeant Rumford. You'll never guess how many guns they got down there. Must be thousands."

"Well, if World War Three breaks out, you'll know where to go, huh, Billy?"

"Yeah, I guess so Jake. Hang on; let me get to another phone so we can talk. "

Jake heard a click, then seconds later another click as Billy picked up the phone. "So what's up?"

"I need some information and I thought maybe you could help."

"Yeah, no problem, Jake. Whadayuh need?"

"Now I don't want to get you into any trouble. But I'd like to find out what info the Department has on the five bodies found shot in the head in the last few months."

"Oh, you mean the ones found in the fields outside of town?"

"Right, Billy those are the ones. Can you dig anything up without getting in trouble?"

"Sure Jake. I file stuff all the time." Billy lowered his voice to a whisper. "Hey Jake, you know a lot of people around here think they're all connected…like maybe a serial killer or something."

"That's why I'd like for you to do a little under-cover work. Are you up for it?"

"Sure I am Jake. Nobody gets to look at all the files like I do." Billy was bragging a bit. "They have me down in the file room all the time puttin' stuff away, or bringin' stuff back up to one of the Detectives or something."

"Sounds like you're a pretty important guy around there, Billy." Jake knew Billy was very proud of the job he did for the Sheriff's Department. "Billy, I'm not going to get you in trouble asking you to do this am I?"

"No problem, Jake," Billy responded. "Shoot, I'm in those files as much as anybody else probably. I'll just sneak in, take a peak, and be out like a ghost. Nobody will know."

"Great Billy. Thanks a lot. Just give me a call at work or at home after you check it out. And if anybody asks...I was calling you about our next fishing trip. Okay?"

"Right Jake. Well, better get back to the job. There's bad guys to bust. Talk to you soon."

As Jake hung up the little yellow incoming call light started blinking on his phone. He grabbed the receiver. "Jake Adams," he answered.

The voice on the other end of the phone could be the voice of God himself, or at least that of James Earl Jones. "Jake Adams...I hear you're looking for me, and that's good, because it's been way too long since I've heard from you. What in the world are you up to?" Mario Franklin had a commanding presence even on the phone.

"Mario, it's great to hear your voice. To be honest I'm looking for some information about a story I'm working on, and you're one of the first people who popped into my mind."

"Sounds intriguing," Mario replied. "I'm gettin' ready to head over to Central Park right now. The sun's poked through the fog and I'll bet there'll be some young men there playin' basketball who should be in school, and I just know the Good Lord wants Mario to talk to them. Why don't you meet me there?"

"Sounds great...I'm headin' out the door now...see you there."

Jake hung up the phone, grabbed his keys, and headed for the door. Mario Franklin was well connected to the local gang scene, whether the gangsters wanted him to be or not. And Jake hoped Mario could get the answer to one simple question...whether the five men who were shot to death were indeed drug dealers.

CHAPTER 7

"So what do we do now…with our Mister Adams?" One of three men stood at a huge floor to ceiling window that overlooked the city. He wore plain black suspenders and a white dress shirt unbuttoned at the top, tie loosened. His pinstriped suit jacket hung on the back of a large high-backed leather chair behind a walnut desk. His hands were cupped one in the other behind his back.

The other two suited men sat in leather armchairs on the other side of the desk. One kept an eye on the man at the window, the other simply looked at the ground.

A short silence followed. Then the man at the window spoke again. "Gentlemen, I'm looking for a little input here."

One of the other men finally spoke up, his words coming out in a very deliberate manner. "Well…we can't just go and kill the most popular T-V anchorman in town. I mean…a bunch of drug dealers is one thing. But I think you could safely say that Jake Adams would be missed around here."

The third man in the room had now gained enough

confidence to speak up. "I still don't know why the woman had to be killed. I think we're piling up way too many bodies in this deal. This is not exactly what I bargained for. And now we're actually sitting here debating whether the most well-known newsman in town should be killed. This is crazy…it's just crazy."

The man at the window walked slowly over to his leather chair and sat down. He laced the fingers of his hands together in front of him on the desk, leaned forward, and stared at the two men across from him.

"Let's get one thing straight. Regardless of what decision we make regarding Mister Adams, we're in this thing together. The plan has been put into action. We all ride this thing out together or we all go down with the ship. Is that understood?"

Both men nodded in response.

The man behind the desk continued. "The Sandoval woman had to be killed. She could tie all of the victims together. And she may have done just that to our Mister Adams. However, at this time it's not clear what, if anything, Mister Adams knows and what he will be able to do with any information he may have received. And yes it's true; it could be a big mistake to remove him at this time. It could create many more problems than it would solve. So, for the time being we'll just leave our Mister Adams alone. After all, there's nothing the Sandoval woman could have told him that would lead him anywhere near us. Does that sound like a logical appraisal of the situation at present?"

"Sounds logical to me."

"Gets my vote."

"Fine." The suspendered man pushed himself away from the desk and returned to the large window. "Mister Adams is off the hook…at least for now."

CHAPTER 8

On his way to Central Park, Jake tried to think just how long he had known Mario Franklin. It must have been fifteen years ago that Mario first called Jake and asked him to emcee a benefit for The East Butterfield Youth Outreach Program. Jake loved doing the community stuff, and he was always glad to lend his name to a good cause. But when he emceed the outreach event, Jake learned a whole new meaning to the term "community service," and it was defined by Mario Franklin. The East Butterfield Youth Center, which was opened because of Mario's hard work, was packed the afternoon Jake showed up to say hi to the kids (mostly Black and Hispanic) and to raffle off a few prizes. Mario was one of the friendliest people he'd ever met, and everyone at the benefit couldn't say enough about how Mario had helped turn so many young people away from gangs and drugs and toward God and community. Jake and Mario immediately knew that they would become good friends as soon as they shook hands that day. It was a friendship that would, forever after, require a big hug every time they met.

Central Park was probably the oldest park in town. It was right in the middle of old town Butterfield, and was considered by even the toughest of gang members to be neutral territory. As Jake approached the park he could see Mario had already arrived. He was easy to spot at six foot seven with a hairless black head and black goatee with several flecks of white. Now in his mid forty's, Mario was still an impressive black man. Over his athletic physique Mario wore khaki pants, a white golf shirt, and white basketball shoes. Mario always stayed in shape to show the young people what a life of Godly living should look like. At present Mario was playing basketball with two young boys who looked to be about thirteen or fourteen. They probably went to one of the local junior high schools, and since this was the middle of the week and the middle of the day, they should have been in class. But it wasn't Mario's style to castigate or lecture. His style was to play the two youngsters in a game of hoops. When the game was over, then came the lecture, which was usually followed by Mario loading the youngsters in his mid-70s Cadillac and taking them back to class.

Jake climbed out of his Jeep and walked toward the basketball court. Mario Franklin was in the act of dunking on the two teenagers. And as the threadbare basketball clanged through the chain link metal net, Mario turned around to see Jake standing at the side of the concrete court.

"Jake." Mario quickly got the two boys attention. "Look here kids…a real life celebrity…and he came all the way down here to help Mario tell you about the importance of God and school."

Jake walked out onto the court and the two men gave each other a huge hug, Jake's head just about facing Mario's sternum. In a much lower voice, Mario said, "It's good to see you Jake, it's been way too long."

"Yeah it sure has," Jake replied, "and I just figured out how the fog finally disappeared today…it's that smile of yours."

"Gotta' be happy, Jake, the Good Lord's in control." Mario turned to the two young men on the court. "You guys shoot around for minute, I'm gonna' talk to my celebrity friend here. He's probably working on some big story and he desperately needs Mario's help." Mario turned to Jake. "Let's go over to one of these picnic tables."

Mario and Jake walked a few feet to an old wooden picnic table that was scarred with years of carvings by people in love or people who had something to communicate to the world that could only be said with a pocketknife. As they sat down, Mario asked, "so what's up Jake…sounded on the phone like this was going to be more than a social visit."

Jake figured it was time to tell the story. Beginning with the discovery of the fifth murder victim, to the late night phone call from the Maria Sandoval, to her revelation that all the victims were drug dealers, to Maria Sandoval's alleged suicide in a pile of cinders that used to be her home.

"So," Jake continued, "I need to find out if all the victims were drug dealers. If that's the case, then their deaths are all linked by a very strong thread…a thread that I know about. And if that means Maria Sandoval didn't commit suicide, then someone also may know that it was me at her house last night. Let's face it…that Red Jeep sticks out like a sore thumb…even in this pea soup."

Mario was deep in thought and after a short pause he asked Jake, "First of all, Jake, tell me what you suspect."

"Everybody in the newsroom thinks the murders are connected somehow. But the cops just say they have no suspects and no leads. But if they are drug related, that means someone out there wanted them dead. It could be local vigilantes in pick-up trucks, it could be rival drug dealers wanting to eliminate the competition."

Mario drew a deep breath and let it out slowly. "Well, if these guys were dealin', I may be able to find out real quick for you."

Mario turned to the two teenagers who had slowed the basketball pace to a leisurely game of HORSE. "Hey, guys, come over here a minute."

Jake was mildly surprised. "The kids?"

"You'd be amazed at what these street kids know," Mario replied.

In a flash, two pairs of Nike basketball shoes were standing in front of Mario.

"Hey, you guys know about the man who was found dead last night?" Mario was trying to sound casual...the kind of information he was trying to get could make the youngsters clam up.

"Yeah," the taller of the two boys piped up..."I heard about it on the radio I think."

Mario continued, "Word on the street is that him and four other men who were murdered recently were all drug dealers...you guys hear anything about that?"

The two teenagers looked at each other, then the taller one gave a suspicious look over at Jake before he turned back to Mario. "Hey, man, this dude's a newsman."

"He's also a good friend of Mario's...and whatever you have to say won't leave this park...you have my word on it."

The two young men looked at each other again before the taller teen turned to talk to Mario and Jake. "Yeah, they were all dealin'. Everybody 'round here knows that. But they weren't just dealin', you know, they were like, big time dealin'. These guys brought in a lot of stuff."

Jake didn't want to alienate the two young men, but he had to wade in with his own questions. "Does anybody think they were all killed *because* they were drug dealers?"

This time the taller of the two young boys looked around the park as if someone might be watching…"You'd better not get me in trouble, man."

"No problem!"

"That ain't what everybody *thinks*, that's what everybody *knows*." The young man now started to sound like he was almost bragging about what he knew. "Somebody wanted those dudes dead."

"Who would want them dead?" asked Jake.

"My mom thinks it's rednecks, you know, those skinhead guys. They hate Black people and Mexicans even though white folks come down here to buy dope all the time."

Now the shorter of the two young boys decided he wanted to get in on the conversation. "Well, some folks think cops killed those guys. Cops hate comin' over here to this side of town. I heard 'em say that if it weren't for gang-bangers and drug dealers this would be a nice town again. I bet they're the ones that want those guys dead."

"But what about other drug dealers…couldn't they have killed them?" Jake asked.

This taller boy took over the conversation again.. "No way man. All the killin' over drugs is usually when some guy's short with the cash, or he's so whacked out on dope he just kills anybody gets in his way. Those guys were makin' a lot of people rich around here. Nobody that liked dope wanted those dudes dead. No man…whoever wasted those dudes planned it out real good."

"Alright…thanks for the info." Jake figured he had what he came for. "And don't worry…nobody will find out we had this talk."

Mario looked at the two young men. "Yeah, thanks for helpin' out a friend...now you two go shoot a few more hoops, then I'm gonna' drag your butts back to school. You get yourselves an education and go to church on Sunday, and you don't wind up dead in some field somewhere."

"Well, Jake, I guess you found out what you came for. What now?"

"I don't know exactly. I've just scratched the surface on this."

"You know," Mario said. "maybe the widow that died did commit suicide. Maybe this isn't as sinister as you're makin' it out to be."

"Yeah, maybe you're right Mario."

"I've got one more guy might give you some information you could use."

"Sure."

"Not the greatest part of town, but since three of the victim's were Hispanic...there's a guy I know may be able to help. Name is Julio. He hangs out at a little bar called El Diablo down on deep Brand."

"El Diablo." Jake had to laugh. "The devil. Sounds like a place you'd love to bring down."

"Oh, I would bring it down Jake, but I get some of my best clients from El Diablo. If you find Julio...just tell him I sent you. You can buy him a beer, but don't shoot pool with him."

"Too bad," Jake said. "I'm pretty good at pool."

"That's the point, Jake." Mario gave Jake a quick wink. "Julio's *not* good at pool...and he hates to lose."

"I get the message." Jake quickly changed his tone of voice. "Mario...I don't think anybody should know about any of this for right now."

"No problem, Jake. Your secret is safe with your friendly neighborhood pastor. And hey, don't wait so long to get in

45

touch. And showing up on Sunday morning wouldn't kill you either. It would be nice to see a shiny white face in the crowd of faithful."

"I promise, Mario."

The two gave each other a big hug. "You'd better get those two to school," Jake said.

"Yeah, I know they just can't wait for Mario's "stay in school" sermon. God bless you, Jake."

"You too...so long."

Jake headed over to his Jeep. Some of his ducks were in a row now, but were those ducks lined up in a carnival shooting gallery, that was the question.

Jake fired up the red Wrangler and headed to a little bar on south Brand Boulevard. The fog was completely burned off now...the sun was high in the sky...and Jake had a date with the devil.

CHAPTER 9

Brand Boulevard is a major business district adjacent to downtown, but as you head south out of town the scenery slowly starts to change. New car showrooms and old established family restaurants give way to auto salvage yards mixed in with farm equipment dealerships. It's a part of town where you can get everything from the bed of a '72 Chevy pickup to new John Deere tractor. The area also starts to take on a decidedly Hispanic flavor. There are taco shops like El Adobe and small family run markets with names like Fiesta Latina. Even the billboards along Brand Boulevard advertise everything from soda pop to cigarettes in Spanish. South Brand Boulevard borders on the beginning of farm country and with a large number of migrant farm workers filling the fields during harvest season, businesses had popped up to take care of their needs. Developers also came into the area to build inexpensive housing and soon south Butterfield was known as Little Mexico. Here, on South Brand, English was a second language, but then the entire population of San Jacinto County was about thirty-five percent Hispanic these days, and the Latino people were a force to be reckoned with, in business and at the ballot box. In fact, in just the past few years, a Hispanic Chamber of Commerce had grown out of the large Mexican business community…and the building that housed The Chamber was on Brand Boulevard, right in the middle of Little Mexico.

Jake Adams was headed to one of those small businesses right now. Probably not one of the gems of the community, but certainly one with a large patronage. El Diablo served cold beer and hot salsa on the jukebox. Combine that with four pool tables and two shuffleboard tables it was an ideal place for the farm workers to congregate after a day in the fields.

As Jake pulled into the dirt and gravel parking lot he noticed four vehicles. Three were pickups, one of those lowered and painted candy-apple red, the other two were work trucks, with rust and mud on the fenders. The fourth vehicle was a '64 Chevy Impala two-door sedan, white on red, with the twin flags of a 327 cubic inch V-8 on the front fender. Jake walked by the Chevy. A look inside showed a four-speed Hurst shifter on the floor…gray and white tuck and rolled interior. Jake would love to look under the hood, but he didn't dare. He wondered which of the four vehicles belonged to Julio, if he was there.

It was just around noon when Jake walked into El Diablo. The sun, which had won today's battle with its nemesis the fog, might as well have gone into full eclipse when Jake stepped through the door. Blinded by the lack of illumination, Jakes other senses took over. The smell of cigarette smoke…the sound of a Mexican song that could have been Country/ Western if it had been in English…and the crisp slap of pool balls…were the only signposts to his surroundings. Jake just stood for a moment, letting his eyes adjust to the lack of light.

The first things that caught Jake's eye were the light bulbs that glowed under round lamp covers hanging directly over the green felt covered pool tables in the back. As his vision shifted over to the bar, two neon signs came into view. One said "Corona" in bright yellow lettering with a green and gold palm tree in the background. The other small neon sign was simpler...a mustard brown oval, with the word "Bohemia" in red in the middle.

The bartender, a stout Mexican gentleman with a toothpick planted firmly in the right side of his mouth, sat on a stool at the far end of the bar. He'd apparently been staring at Jake since he walked in. As he looked around, Jake saw that others in the bar had been taking notice of the obviously Caucasian man in the doorway. It reminded Jake of Mario's line, "a shiny white face in the middle of all the faithful."

Jake walked in, his eyes now growing accustomed to the darkness, and figured he'd take a tip from the neon. "I'll have a Bohemia," Jake said in his best flat monotone voice. Mexican food was one of Jake's favorites, so he knew that the pronunciation of the brew was...*bo-ay'-mia*...and he figured that should count for at least a few points with the burly bartender. It was hard to tell. The barkeep popped the top on the brown bottle of brew and slid it down the bar toward Jake.

Jake grabbed the beer in mid-flight, took a swallow, and walked down to the end of the bar to get right to the business at hand.

He tried to look friendly but not too friendly. "I'm lookin' for a guy named Julio...Mario Franklin said I might be able to find him here."

"Oh, is that what Mario said?" replied the bartender staring straight at Jake.

Jake said nothing. After a short pause...the beefy bartender did. "You're the news guy ain't ya'? What the heck you want with Julio?"

"Just a couple of questions…and I'm not here as a news guy. Mario said maybe Julio could help me out. If not, that's okay. I can drink my beer and go."

Jake's sincerity and brevity seemed to work…"Julio's back there…last table" The bartender tilted his head toward the back of the barroom.

Jake took a pull from his bottle of beer and walked toward the pool tables, past two Hispanic men in dirty jeans and tee shirts who were in the middle of a game of eight ball. At the very back table, Jake saw a lone figure who was moving around the pool table like was stalking prey. He had the butt of the cue stick in his right hand, turning it as he chalked up the tip with his left. Julio was massive. He wasn't that tall, but he was obviously a body builder, with the physique of the Incredible Hulk. He was wearing black jeans and a black tank top. He had a moustache and a goatee, and his hair, which was pulled back into a ponytail, hung down past his shoulders. He never looked up as Jake approached.

"Are you Julio?" No reply. "My name's Jake Adams. Mario Franklin said you might be able to help me. He said I might find you here."

Julio finally looked up…but just stared at Jake. He reached over to a small table by the wall and grabbed a long neck bottle of Budweiser and took a pull. "Well, half of what Mario told you is true. The other half depends on what you want. You're the guy on T-V, huh?"

"Yeah," said Jake. "but I'm not here on a news story. It's more…well…it's kind of personal." Jake figured Julio wasn't the type to beat around the bush in a conversation so neither did Jake. "It's about the five men who were shot in the back of the head and left in the fields around town over the past few months. I hear they were all drug dealers."

"Sounds like you're working on a story to me!"

"But I'm not. It's just that the wife of the last victim called me the night the body was found. I talked to her an hour before she was found burned to death in her home."

"Maria called you?"

"You know Maria Sandoval?" asked Jake.

"Maybe." Julio took another pull on his beer.

"The authorities say she committed suicide."

"Suicide my ass!" Julio shot back, and he started stalking the pool table again.

"What do you mean by that?"

"Just what I said...you shouldn't believe everything you read in the papers."

"I don't, but I promised Maria Sandoval I would try to find out who killed her husband."

Julio tried a corner pocket shot and missed. "You promised huh? You know, you might not like what you find."

"All I know is Maria Sandoval asked me to help. And if she didn't commit suicide, then whoever killed her may have seen me leave her house. So I honor my promise to Maria, and maybe I save my own ass in the process."

Julio didn't respond, and Jake suddenly felt himself getting impatient and a little angry. "I'm not on a news story. But if you can't help, then thanks anyway. I'm sorry I wasted your time."

Julio tossed the cue stick down on the green felt of the pool table. He placed both hands palms down on the side of the table, and leaned forward staring at Jake underneath the glare of the light that hung over the center of the table. "Okay, news guy, here you go...and take notes 'cause I ain't sayin' this twice. Yeah, all the dead guys were dealin'. And yeah, Maria was probably killed 'cause she talked to you. These ain't just murders man, they're hits. And the drugs, man, they just keep comin' in. So, a lot of dead dealers but still lots of drugs. That enough for you?"

"You mean it's rival drug dealers?"

"You're from the wrong side of town man or what I just told you would have already sunk in. But I ain't spellin' it out. You gotta' do some work on your own. But I will tell you where to start. Old Town Butterfield, where the Crosstown Freeway goes over Center Street…by the Rescue Mission, underneath the overpass. You check it out some night…three…maybe four in the morning. You get lucky you'll see what I mean…and maybe that'll give you something to investigate."

Julio grabbed the cue stick from the pool table and gave Jake another stare. He put the pool cue back in the wall rack, grabbed the bottle of Bud and finished it off. "Conversation's over. You got your information…but one thing…you don't mention my name. You get me killed in all this and I'm gonna' be real pissed…okay?"

"Yeah, no problem," Jake replied.

"Now get outta' here…news is over." Julio walked past Jake to the bar. "'Gimme another" he called to the bartender.

Jake found himself at a total loss for words. He had his information, but now what to do with it. He started walking. As he reached Julio he just stopped for a brief second and said "thanks" and kept on walking…right out the door into the blinding sunlight.

CHAPTER 10

Jake could only shake his head as he drove the red Jeep back to town. If the Hulk-like Julio was telling the truth, this investigation Jake had gotten himself involved in had just taken a major turn. It looked like the next logical step, if there was anything logical about Jake's life right now, was a stakeout. And for a late-night stakeout to be successful, Jake figured he'd better make a stop at another local tavern...one with which Jake was much more familiar.

The Dog House was right in the middle of downtown Butterfield. It stood as somewhat of a monument to the durability of the area. The Dog House was located in one of a dozen or so buildings that had survived the earthquake of 1952. In fact the inside walls of the old bar were covered with pictures of the aftermath of the quake. The temblor had measured something over seven, and the giant rolling quake had left most of the downtown area in rubble. One of the survivors was the Dog House, which was on the bottom floor of the old Palomar Hotel. The Palomar, built back in the 20s, was the crown jewel of downtown in that era. People of wealth traveling up and down the valley often stayed at the Palomar. With its thick rich carpeting and garish chandeliers, it was a tribute to the oil barons and farm owners of that time who had made their fortunes in the rich earth of the San Jacinto Valley. One of the largest farmers of the day, John Palomar, had built the hotel. Palomar land was still being farmed by various descendents, growing everything from cotton to grapes to almonds. But John Palomar's hotel had not only fallen from family hands, it had fallen on hard times. The only tenants it housed now were the down and out…the outcasts of society who needed a month-to-month crash pad they could use as a permanent address to collect their welfare and disability checks.

What was now The Dog House, used to be the Palomar Club. The Palomar Club…whose walls were once adorned with oil paintings of racehorses, beautiful women in long dresses and large lacy hats and parasols, and pictures of large lakes filled with swans at sunset, was now the Dog House. The fine paintings had been replaced by scores of pictures of the '52 quake and the devastation it caused in downtown Butterfield. The pictures of what the quake left behind were a fitting tribute to what the bar had now become, just a small hole-in-the-wall tavern. The only thing that kept it alive was the patronage of a solid flood of the local working class, many of whom wore hard hats or rode Harley-Davidsons. And since Jake hated the neckties he had to put on each day, he felt right at home in the Dog House. Jake had also come to know the owner over the years, a rotund bearded Vietnam veteran who had rescued the old bar from the cobwebs years ago and had brought it back to life in its current incarnation.

Rick Rollins had been the one who helped put the local Vietnam veterans on the map in Butterfield. He'd started the local Vietnam Veterans Association, attracting a host of hardened Vets who preferred to steer clear of the VFW crowd. Rollins had also made sure that the Vietnam veterans and their wives and families were a proud part of each year's Veteran's Day Parade through the streets of downtown Butterfield. Whenever there was a story about the Vietnam War to cover, you always saw a sound bite from Rick Rollins. The only pictures on the wall other than those of the earthquake were of Rick Rollins in uniform, in the Army, in Vietnam. Rick made no apologies for the war, and was proud he had served. The only regret he had was that the U-S didn't *kick ass* right to the very end.

A big fancy bar would never have been in Rick Rollins entrepreneurial plans, just a bar where he was comfortable, and one that could cater to the people he envisioned himself fighting for when he was a soldier.

Jake met Rick years ago. The bar was close to work, which meant it was also close to home. And since the bar was more his style than many of the other more stylish pubs in downtown, he often stopped in after the late shift for a cold one before heading home. Jake and Rick had become good friends. Jake, too, had served in the military during the Vietnam era, although he never actually served in Vietnam. After a number of his buddies had been drafted into the Army, Jake decided to join the Air Force. While carrying a weapon into war wasn't exactly his thing, he did want to serve his country. So in the summer of 1967, Jake raised his right hand and headed to basic training in Amarillo, Texas.

Because of that military service, Rick had asked Jake to emcee a number of benefits and fundraisers for Rick's Vietnam Vets Association, and Jake had come to have a great deal of respect for Rick's "live and let live attitude." Now Jake would be calling on their friendship in a slightly different way.

As Jake walked into The Dog House he wasn't met with the total blackout he had experienced at El Diablo. The Dog House had plenty of light inside. Not too bright of course…but Rick thought that the old-fashioned carriage lamps along the walls, burning with low wattage bulbs, added a rustic ambiance to the place. He was also smart enough to know his clientele. The more light, the less hanky panky. Downtown Butterfield was perfectly capable of attracting its share of nefarious characters…and when they were thirsty, they usually headed for The Dog House.

As Jake walked through the large swinging double doors, Rick Rollins was sitting behind the bar on a stool doing what he usually did before the afternoon early birds showed up; a crossword puzzle.

"Hey Jake…it's a bit early in the day for you isn't it?" Rick stood up and smiled. He stretched his burly arm over the bar…Jake grabbed his hand and gave it a solid shake. Rick had a full but well trimmed beard and moustache, which had remained its natural reddish brown through the years. His hair hung down the back of his neck, looking like he'd missed a few haircuts.

"Yeah, too early for a brew," Jake replied, "but not too early for some help from and old friend." Jake sat on a barstool across the bar from Rick.

"An old friend?" Rick gave Jake a sideways sarcastic look. "Sounds like a con job comin' on to me."

"Very funny Rick. Truth is, I do have a favor to ask."

"I don't loan money and I don't run tabs. Anything else is up for negotiation. Fire away."

"Okay." Jake suddenly felt a little embarrassed by the question he was about to ask. "I need to borrow your car…"

"Borrow my car?" Rick gave Jake an incredulous look.

"What do you want with my old clunker...you drive a fairly new Jeep as I recall."

Rick Rollins drove a 1966 Mustang. It was a clean little car, one that Rick had every intention in the world of fixing up someday...problem is, someday just never came. Not that the Mustang was in bad shape. The 289 cubic inch V-8 ran great and the automatic transmission worked fine. The body was in good shape except for a few door dings. The faded blue paint was original. The interior was also original, which meant the bucket seats and the carpeting were a bit worn. Rick had always envisioned a shiny new paint job, new rims, refurbished interior, and lots of chrome on the engine. Unfortunately, as the Rolling Stones song goes, "You can't always get what you want." Rick still loved the car though, and he would be the first to admit that the Mustang cost him a lot less just the way it was.

"That's the problem," Jake replied. "My red Jeep sort of stands out in a crowd. I need something a little more... well...inconspicuous if you know what I mean."

"What are you gonna' do, rob a bank? Gonna' use my old Mustang as a getaway car. Why don't I just come along for the ride? I'll be your wheel man."

A huge grin crept over Jake's face. "Yeah, you and me...Butch Cassidy and the Sundance Kid...that's a laugh. No I'm serious. I have to do something...and my Jeep is just too loud. I wish I could tell you about it, but I just can't right now."

"Yeah, yeah, I know the next line. If you tell me you'll have to kill me, right?" Rick shrugged his shoulders. "Sure what they hay. Of course I get to use your Jeep, right?"

"You bet...you can do a little four wheelin'. Go climb a mountain or something."

"Jake, my friend, it's all I can do to climb out of bed in the morning. Climbing a mountain might be a little out of my league. But I might look pretty cool drivin' a red Jeep around town"

Rick stood up, reached into his pocket and pulled out a set of keys. Taking the Mustang's key off the ring he slapped it down on the hardwood bar. "There you go...she's parked right out here in the alley. When do I get 'er back?"

Jake took the Jeep key off his key ring and slid it over to Rick. "Depends on when I get done with what I need to get done...I'll be back in tomorrow. The Jeep is parked across the street in the lot."

"Take good care of her," Rick said as he gave Jake a mock mournful look.

"Yeah...just like you do," Jake shot back.

Rick shook his head and gave Jake a smile. "Good luck with whatever."

Jake smiled back. "Thanks buddy, I really do appreciate this. Someday I'll tell you all about it." Jake headed out the large double swinging doors and down the alley to the old Mustang. He unlocked the door, slid behind the wheel, put the key in the ignition and gave it a turn. The engine roared to life, and Jake pulled out of the alley and headed to work. Sitting in the old faded blue Mustang was a far cry from riding high in his bright red Jeep. And Jake felt a small part of his mission was accomplished. He felt truly incognito.

CHAPTER 11

Back in the Eyewitness Newsroom the first thing on Jake's mind was making a quick search for Karen Foley. The Sandoval case was Karen's story. Whatever questions needed to be asked, Karen would ask them. So, Jake went in search of the Eyewitness News star reporter.

Karen had been out most of the day with cameraman Phil Cannon, first in the field southwest of town where the body of Rudy Sandoval had been found, then over to what remained of the Sandoval house on Orchard Court. Karen would have a live report from Orchard Court on the six o'clock show, and she was in the edit booth now, jotting down notes in shorthand on a lined yellow legal pad, as she looked intently at the video that spelled out the sequence of events that took the lives of two people. First Karen would pick out the video she would use to tell the story, and then she would lay down her voice track on a separate tape, describing the deadly events of last evening, from the discovery of Rudy Sandoval's body to the fiery death of Maria Sandoval. Karen's own narrative would be combined with sound bites from a spokesperson from the Sheriff's Department and a resident in the neighborhood where the Sandoval house went up in flames. Then Phil Cannon, would take the raw video, the sound bites, and Karen's voice track, and edit them together into a two-minute package. With a little creative editing, you would actually see Karen walk out of the empty field and into the charred ruins of the home where Maria Sandoval's body had been found.

As Jake approached the edit booth, he saw Karen through the glass door, microphone in hand, recording her voice track. He waited until she was done, and he gently tapped on the glass door. Karen turned around and gave Jake a smile and waved at him to come in. Jake slid the glass door open. "Busy day, huh?"

"Oh...it's been crazy...a lot of running around...why couldn't these two people have died together. It would sure make my job a lot easier."

"So what's the deal?" Jake would try to get Karen's slant on the story without giving away anything that he knew. "This is the fifth body. Sheriff's Department still saying they're not connected?"

"Well," Karen shook her head and thought for a second. "They're still sticking to the same old story line...no motive, no suspects. But I asked them point blank if five men shot in the back of the head in five different fields outside of town didn't look connected to them. The Sheriff's Commander just said they didn't have any evidence to that effect at the time. You'll hear his sound bite tonight. He said it could be gang related or something, but they don't know." Karen turned around and hit the eject button on the tape machine. "You know, they may know a lot more than they're telling us right now, and they just don't want it to be public knowledge. Lord knows they've done that before. We may not know anything 'till they have a suspect in custody."

"But what about Sandoval's widow? I heard that it may not have been suicide at all."

Karen walked out of the edit booth with Jake following behind. "I don't know where you heard that, but if it wasn't suicide, then Commander Collins sure sounds convincing. Apparently the Sheriff's Deputy who went over to give the widow the bad news last night said that she took it really hard…got hysterical and everything. I guess he even offered to stay with her for a while until she calmed down, but she said no."

Jake knew that wasn't the way Maria Sandoval told the story the night before, but again, that was information that Jake would have to keep to himself for now.

"Well, thanks for the info, Karen. You gonna' be live at Orchard Court tonight?"

"You've got a good memory for street names…yeah, that's where we'll be. Heck of a street name for what happened there."

"Sure is." Jake walked back over to his desk. He had Eyewitness News at Six and Eleven to get through before he went on his late night surveillance mission to one of the seedier sides of Butterfield.

CHAPTER 12

It seemed like an eternity, but Eyewitness News at eleven was finally over. Jake started getting nervous about his after midnight mission shortly before the eleven o'clock news began. His co-anchor, Lisa Kraft, had even mentioned that Jake looked a little preoccupied. Jake just laughed and shrugged it off, blaming it on senility. He figured at nearly sixty years of age, if he was old enough to get mail from the AARP, he was old enough to use his age as an excuse for his occasionally odd behavior. It rarely worked, but Jake had fun doing it.

Jake said a few quick goodnights, and headed out to Rick Rollins' Mustang…fired it up and headed home to get ready for his late night adventure. It looked like the weather was giving him a break. A small front was moving through the area. A southerly breeze was blowing the leaves and dust around. But most importantly, the wind was clearing out the fog and warming the air enough to make his late night vigil more comfortable and a lot more visible. If he was going to try and spot a drug deal going down during the usually foggy winter in Butterfield, Jake figured he had at least picked the right night.

At home, a sense of excitement began to creep into the anxiety over what lay ahead, and Jake decided if he was going to go "undercover" he might as well look the part. He went to his dresser and grabbed a pair of black jeans and a long sleeved black turtleneck golf shirt. He then went to the closet and rummaged around for an old pair of black Nike high top basketball shoes that he thought were in there with all the other stuff that should have gone to the Goodwill a long time ago. After he located the shoes, Jake started searching around the shelves above the clothes hangars to find an old navy blue knit stocking hat that had a Dallas Cowboys logo on it. He found the hat and proceeded to dress for the occasion. He pulled on the black jeans, slid the black long sleeved turtleneck over his head, and laced up the black basketball shoes. He then stretched the knit stocking cap over his head and went to the full-length mirror on the back of his bedroom door and stared at himself for a moment. Slowly a grin crept over Jake's face as he shook his head at what he saw. "Heck," Jake thought to himself…"maybe Rick Rollins was right…maybe I should be knocking over a bank…or at least a local convenience store."

"Okay," Jake thought to himself. "Straighten up. This is serious. Even if this turns out to be a wild goose chase, it's something you have to do, maybe for a few nights in a row…however long it takes, to either find the big bad drug dealers, or decide that you're wasting your time. Either way, you've gone this far, may as well finish it out."

Jake looked at his watch…it was 12:30. Time to go.

* * *

Center Street is just a little northeast of downtown Butterfield. At the turn of the century, Center Street was a major hub of activity for the area because of the railroad. Cotton and carrots…tycoons and tourists…they were all transported by train…and when the train stopped in Butterfield, it stopped at Center Street Station. In those days it didn't take long for some of the areas entrepreneurs to see Center Street as a prime real estate location. In a short time everything from hotels to taverns were popping up along Center Street. And that was quickly followed by hookers and gamblers and the like. Center Street Station was a great jumping-off place to do a little business, and then get on a train and head to the next town.

But the Center Street boom would only last until around 1940. Travel by train gradually gave ground to cars and airplanes. And the city fathers had decided that there was too much sin surrounding the Center Street Station, so Downtown Butterfield was officially re-located a couple of miles away to the southeast. That's where the Courthouse and the Sheriff's Department were built. And that's where the local merchants decided to set up shop as well. It's also where the new railroad station would eventually be built.

Center Street was now just a rundown shell of what it used to be. The high rollers of the turn of the century had been replaced by the homeless and the hobos. The warehouses that used to hold everything from dry goods to furniture were now empty and weather-warn. The only sign of life on the deserted street was the Butterfield Rescue Mission. The mission was known for it's friendly staff, its' hot meals, and its' fire and brimstone preaching by Father Donald Durbin. A meal and a bed for the night were always free to the indigent. But suppertime at the Mission was also preachin' time. And Father Durbin was one of the best. God had a plan for each and every person taking advantage of the Lord's generosity, and it was their responsibility to take advantage of the Mission's connections in the community so they could get back on their feet and start contributing to society. Father Durbin was also good at preachin' to local businessmen about donating to the Mission. "Padre Don," as he was called, was a master at both saving the lost and filling the community collection plate. Scores of success stories...turning the down-and-out into upstanding, tax paying citizens of Butterfield ensured that Father Durbin always had enough money to keep the Mission doors open, and the bright red neon cross burning on the front of the Mission. It was the crimson cloud of light from that neon cross that Jake Adams now saw from a few blocks away.

The Rescue Mission was about a half a block from the end of Center Street which dead ended at the railroad tracks. The trains didn't stop there anymore. They just rolled slowly through. A huge chain-link fence had been erected at the end of the street and along the railroad tracks after a number homeless people had fallen asleep drunk on the tracks and had been run over by the passing trains. The old Center Street Station building itself had been moved to the San Jacinto County Museum some twenty years ago. The only signs of life on the old street now were the homeless that frequented the area by day, and the bright red neon cross that lit up the sky at night.

Directly across the street to the north, were the naked concrete signs of progress that had invaded Center Street...huge pylons that supported the Crosstown Freeway, which had been built back in the '70s. When the weather was warmer, it wouldn't be unusual to see some of the homeless spending the night under the freeway overpass. A host of threadbare couches and chairs decorated the area...making the darkened area look like a furniture graveyard. An abundance of other junk also littered the area...much of it the remains of makeshift shelters. It was the refuse of life, all accumulated by people who, themselves, had become the refuse of their own society. All this junk rested on an expanse of dirt and gravel that went on into the darkness underneath the freeway overpass as it trekked on to the north. It would be this dirt and gravel area that would be Jake's focus tonight.

Jake drove toward the light of the neon cross like a moth to a flame. He checked his watch...one a.m. He wheeled the Mustang quietly into the parking lot of the Mission. Two vehicles were parked there. One belonged to whoever had night duty at the Mission. The other was an old Chevy window van with Butterfield Rescue Mission painted in faded red paint on the side. Jake pulled into a spot on the other side of the van, put the Mustang in park, and shut off the engine. He grabbed a thermos of coffee from the passenger's seat and climbed into the back where he'd stashed a couple of blankets and a pillow. He rolled down the right side window a few inches to get a little ventilation and a better sense of the sounds around him. He then stretched out in the back seat, facing the overpass.

The light from the red neon cross washed across the street, splashing off the sides of the concrete pillars...and trying desperately to fill the darkness underneath the freeway. The moon was full and high overhead, and Jake figured anything that went on within a hundred yards or so would be at least somewhat visible.

As Jake continued his stealth-like surveillance of the surrounding terrain, he was also busy downing the last of his coffee. After about an hour Jake began to question the validity and the sanity of this late night stakeout. And once the uncertainty started to settle in, so did the fatigue. He found himself scrunching down in the seat a little further as he chugged the last of the coffee, struggling to keep his eyelids open.

The cup was still at his lips when Jake heard the first sounds of the night, which quickly sent his senses into high gear. It was the sound of a car coming down Center Street. A few seconds went by, and finally the light from someone's high beams started to fill the street in front of him. Jake's eyes were now wide open as he focused on what was quickly coming into view. He tried not to move a muscle. The only things that moved were his eyeballs as he followed a compact car as it slowly rolled by. On the side of the car, in bright red and yellow lettering, was a logo…Shaw Security. Jake had no idea that rent-a-cops would be patrolling the area, nor did he know how often they would come around. He watched as the small car rolled out of view past the Mission; he heard it make a U-turn at the end of the street, and he watched it roll slowly by in the other direction. It took just a couple of minutes, and the car was gone. Apparently Shaw Security felt that all was well on Center Street at two in the morning.

"Great," Jake thought to himself. "If this security guy is a regular on the beat, what's the chance of me seeing a drug deal tonight…or any other night for that matter? Julio must be laughing his head off," Jake thought, "knowing that his barroom advice has me parked at the Rescue Mission in the middle of the night waiting for the big bad boogie man." Jake had a definite urge to climb back in the front seat, fire up the Mustang, and head home.

Instead Jake figured since he was already here, covered in blankets in the backseat, he might as well stick it out a while longer. So, with the quiet of the Butterfield night surrounding him, he rearranged the pillow behind his head, pulled a blanket up around his neck, and settled in. And after about half an hour of fending off the sandman, Jake's eyelids finally gave in under the weight…and he drifted off to sleep.

His nap was short-lived. Suddenly Jake's eyes were wide open as a flood of light filled the Mustang. At first Jake thought someone was shining a flashlight into the car. Maybe someone who worked at the Mission wanted to know just what Jake was doing there crashed out in the back seat. In the split second surrounding Jake's rude awakening, he was already devising his explanation to whoever was holding what had to be a flashlight with some really big batteries. But just as Jake was about to raise his head above window level, the light quickly moved away. As he peered out the window Jake saw where the light was coming from. Another car now occupied the street in front of the Mission…a large, late model sedan. Someone inside the sedan was using a spotlight to check out the area. The beam of light swung away from the mission…down the street toward the train tracks…then across the street, doing a thorough search of the debris filled dirt and gravel area underneath the freeway. The beam of light then swung around back up Center Street. Suddenly the light went dark, but just as quickly it came back on, stayed on for a split second, then it was off again. The driver then turned off the headlights and took a sharp left, heading into the dirt and gravel area underneath the freeway. No sooner had the sedan moved off into the darkness than another vehicle came into view up Center Street. A full sized panel van, headlights already out, followed the sedan into the darkness of the freeway overpass.

Jake's heart was pounding, and he knew it was time to take action. This could be what he came for. This is why he put on the ridiculous black outfit that made him look like some midnight ninja.

"Here we go," Jake thought to himself as he rolled down the Mustang's window the rest of the way. Reaching out, he grabbed the edge of the roof with both hands, and quietly pulled himself out through the open window. A quick assessment of the situation made Jake's next move clear. Going directly across the street into the sea of red neon was obviously out of the question, so Jake headed to the back of the Mission where an alley led toward the tracks a half block away. A few steps later another problem quickly revealed itself. The chain link fence that kept the drunks off the tracks was also keeping Jake from getting to the tracks so he could stalk his prey from a discreet vantage point. "Why hadn't he thought of this chain link chink in his armor earlier?" Jake thought to himself. He was about to retrace his steps to look for an alternate route when he noticed a break in the fence. Someone had pushed the fence up near one of the metal posts, creating an opening large enough squeeze through. The opening's creator was most likely one of the hobos who grabbed a free ride in and out of town in a boxcar, but who also liked the free bed and board of the Mission. Kneeling down on all fours, Jake carefully crawled through the opening, standing up on the other side and quietly dusting himself off.

Being on the other side of the fence made all the difference. The fence was now between him and his late night visitors. High grass and weeds had grown up along the fence over the winter, which would help muffle his footsteps, and combined with an array of old furniture, cardboard boxes and warped plywood, the fence line provided perfect cover.

Jake stepped stealthily on the balls of his feet as he made his way along the fence line making sure not to set his foot down on anything that would signal his presence. As Jake approached the vehicles, he could see two men already standing at the back of the van. They whispered in hushed tones making their words unintelligible. Jake found a spot along the fence with a number of old cardboard boxes leaning up against it, and decided that was as far as he needed to go. Jake stuck his head out just far enough from behind the cardboard to see one of the men open the back doors of the van. Unluckily, no interior light came on. And though the moon had disappeared from sight at this late hour, there were enough streetlights in the general area to help with Jake's vision, which had become accustomed to the darkened surroundings. Then the other man opened up the trunk of the large sedan. Jake was in luck…the trunk light came on. Immediately, both men looked around as if the light had startled them. A few short words, and one of the man walked over and started unloading some large packages from the van, while the other man reached for the trunk and quickly removed the bulb. Once again there was darkness. He could barely see the two shadowy figures, but he could hear the two men as they moved the packages from the van to the trunk of the car. He heard the trunk of the car quietly pushed shut, and then the double doors of the van were silently shut as well. A few more whispered words and suddenly the glow of a small flashlight appeared. The focus of the dim light was an envelope. The man at the back of the sedan held the light, the other man pulled money out of the envelope and counted it in silence. Just as suddenly, the light was extinguished. The two men parted company. Car doors were opened, a quick glimpse of an interior light in the sedan, and the doors were shut again, and the engines of the van and the sedan sprang to life.

The van led the way back to Center Street, neither driver using headlamps. As the large white sedan pulled parallel with his location, Jake figured it was time to get a better glimpse of the vehicles if at all possible. He ran, half hunched over, trying to stay just behind and out of sight of the sedan as it followed the van out from underneath the overpass. As the van made a right onto the pavement, the headlights remained dark. But as the sedan entered Center Street, its headlights suddenly illuminated the street ahead. But more importantly for Jake, who'd kept within fairly close proximity to the departing car, the light around the rear license plate came on as well. And just before the sedan full of precious cargo finished it's right turn onto Center Street, Jake got a solid look at the license plate number.

With the two vehicles gone, Jake made his way back through the hole in the fence, and back to the Mustang. He would let the panel van and the white sedan get far from Center Street before he would venture out of the area. Jake was wired. His mind was racing. His hands and face were chilled from the night air. He didn't have a drop of coffee to warm him now, but he didn't care. He had what certainly looked like a drug deal going down…and better yet…he had a license plate number. Not bad work for a wild goose chase in the middle of the night.

CHAPTER 13

The first thing that caught Jake's half-opened eyes in the morning was the clock on the night stand. He couldn't believe it. The numbers on the clock said 11:23. When he'd hit the sack it was about four in the morning. Jake figured a short sleep would get him up around eight. But he'd forgotten one important thing…setting the alarm. And he hadn't gauged the toll the last two nights had taken on him. He'd slept soundly, but now he was awake, and the next bit of business Jake had to attend to was sitting on the nightstand right next to the clock that now read 11:24. It was a piece of paper with a license plate number hastily scribbled on it. Jake had written down the number while sitting in the Mustang in the parking lot of the Rescue Mission. He was still in his all-black spy attire, except for the black Nike's that were lying on the floor beside the bed. His first move was to grab the piece of paper and open it to make sure he'd really written down the number, make sure he hadn't just awakened from some bizarre news anchor dream. The number was there. He climbed out of bed, and slowly made his way to the kitchen to nuke a cup of coffee and make a phone call.

While the cup of water was in the microwave, Jake went to a desk in the living room and found a small address book that loosely corresponded with his Rolodex at work. The buzzer on the microwave made its usual irritating sound. Jake grabbed the cup of hot water and added instant coffee and non-fat milk. After a brisk stirring, he took a gulp of the brew and started thumbing through the address book.

Under "C" Jake found the name of Shelly Crook. Jake took the cordless phone from the cradle on the wall and punched in Shelley Crook's work number…put the phone to his ear and took another large swallow of coffee.

"Department of Motor Vehicles," a friendly voice came on the line. "How may we help you?"

"Shelly Crook please," Jake said using his best phone manners.

A recorded voice filled the void telling him of the many services the DMV now offered. Shortly, a pleasant voice came on the line. "This is Ms. Crook."

"Hello Ms. Crook…this is Mr. Adams," Jake said in a very formal tone of voice.

Shelly apparently hadn't caught on yet. "Yes, and how may we help you Mr. Adams?"

"Well," Jake returned to his normal voice. "You can start by calling me Jake."

"Jake!!!…what the…how the heck are you? Long time, no see…or hear…or whatever." Shelly sounded a bit flustered, but very happy to hear Jake's voice on the other end of the phone.

"I'm fine…can you talk?"

"Sure…what's up?"

Jake and Shelly had known each other for some time. They had dated about three years ago. They met at a local Law

Enforcement Day that was put on each year, for the younger kids, as the school year began. The Sheriff's Department and other agencies put on a fall get-together at a local park so the young students could feel comfortable around cops, and get an idea of how to take advantage of some of the local services that were available to the kids and their parents. But mostly it was a public relations project to show local law enforcement and other emergency services in a friendly and favorable light. One of the booths that always set up was from the DMV. They were there to show students who were approaching driving age how to best go about getting their driver's license. Shelly, being one of the new recruits to the DMV, was responsible for manning the booth, answering questions, and handing out brochures. Jake was the emcee for the day, and that's where he'd met Shelly.

She was probably twenty years younger than Jake, but a short debate on the pros and cons of the safety of four-wheeling on the back roads of San Jacinto County eventually led to Jake taking Shelly for a tour of one of his favorite back road spots. What started out as something of a dare, turned into six months of dating…if you could call it that. Jake loved Shelly's youthful exuberance…and Shelly found that she loved being in the great outdoors, in the company of Jake's rather off center sense of humor. Jake always joked that he was old enough to be Shelly's father…and on one late August adventure to a small lake hidden at the top of one of Jake's favorite mountaintop retreats, that theory was put to the test.

Shelly had packed a picnic lunch…and Jake had brought along a couple of bottles of not-too-expensive wine in the ice chest. Jake was trying his gentlemanly best to teach Shelly how to thread a worm onto a hook, and since Shelly couldn't have cared less about fishing, they both settled in on the macaroni salad and tuna fish sandwiches that Shelly had packed in a wicker basket...washed down by Sauvignon Blanc. As Jake was rummaging around in the picnic basket for the corkscrew to open the second bottle of wine...Shelly suddenly made a passionate pass at the silver haired anchorman. The result of that kiss wasn't exactly what either one would have imagined...they both broke out laughing. Not that the kiss was poorly delivered or received. But after all the father-daughter talk from Jake, and after all the "buddying" around the two had done...suddenly, the kiss...while seemingly appropriate at the time...became totally out of place. And once Jake and Shelly had stopped laughing, Jake looked at Shelly and said, "well...guess you can lead a horse to wine...but you don't know what the hell he's going to do after that."

It wasn't much of a joke...but it summed up the fact that...even though Jake and Shelly had a great friendship...a friendship would be as far as the relationship would go.

It wasn't long after Shelly realized that Jake was indeed a "father figure" that she met up with a young Highway Patrolman who came into the DMV occasionally on business. His name was Mick Williams. He was the Public Information Officer, or the P.I.O. as the media called him, for the local Highway Patrol. Shelly and Mick had been going together for over two years now. Jake knew Mick well. He talked with him live on the air every time there was a fatal accident out on the interstate or a big drug bust, usually involving people who were just passing through Butterfield on the highway, but who had the misfortune of having a tail-light out and far too much marijuana in the trunk. In fact, Jake and Mick had become solid golfing buddies. And usually, after every round of golf...Jake would head to Mick's house for a cold one...and the person popping the tops on the brewskies was Shelly. Small towns made for some interesting friendships, and Jake had certainly experienced his share.

So Jake felt perfectly comfortable when he got right to the point. "Shell…I need a favor."

"I didn't figure you were calling for a date…how can I help."

Jake paused for a moment…he didn't want to ask Shelly for something that could get her in trouble…"If you can…and say no if you can't…can you run down a license plate number for me?"

Jake heard a short exhale of air on the other end…he didn't realize it was a stifled laugh…"Can I do what??" Shelly tried to sound serious. "What do you think this is the DMV?"

"Very funny," Jake replied.

"Sorry Jake," Shelly said. "Sure I can help."

"If I give you a license plate number, what can you tell me about it. I mean how much information?"

"Well," Shelly was trying to sound pensive. "If you give me *your* license plate number, I think the DMV can tell you what you had for dinner last night. Big Brother you know."

"I don't think cold left-over pizza is the information we're looking for…but I do have a license plate number…and I would just love to find out who it belongs to."

"Information is my business," Shelly responded. "And when it comes to license plates…we know more about 'em than the convicts who made 'em…fire away."

"Okay." Jake was staring at his crumpled piece of paper…suddenly feeling like he was about to climb on an "E" ticket ride at Magic Mountain…"1-S-U-B-7-2-7."

"1SUB727," Shelly replied. Jake heard the clicking of computer keys…a pause…a few more taps on the keyboard… and then, "wow…caught yourself a big one Jake…County plate."

"What do you mean, County plate?" Jake was suddenly confused, not prepared for the answer Shelly had given him.

"County plate. The car is registered to San Jacinto County." Shelly replied in a very matter-of-fact tone.

Jake gathered his puzzled thoughts together. "I thought government vehicles said exempt on the plate."

"Only some of them," replied Shelly. "Law enforcement...dog catchers...that kind of stuff. But a lot of County officials and under cover cops don't want to be labeled with an exempt plate...so they use the regular plates. More discreet, if you know what I mean."

"I know what you mean...but if this is a County vehicle...can you tell me who drives it?"

"Hang on." Jake heard the tapping of more computer keys. "Sorry, Jake. It's a white Chevrolet Caprice...but it's just registered to the County...it doesn't say who's actually driving it. County administration probably divvies them up...you'd have to check the County Admin offices. But I'm guessing they'll be pretty tight-lipped about it."

"Okay...thanks Shelly. Guess I'll see you tomorrow afternoon...me and your significant other are playing golf in the morning."

"Yeah, I know." Shelly gave off a half-hearted laugh. "I wish Mick looked forward to seeing me like he looks forward to playing golf with you."

"I promise I won't take all his money tomorrow, if that'll make you feel better."

"Just leave him enough so he can take me out to dinner."

Jake laughed. "Deal. Thanks Shelly. I mean it. You're the greatest."

"Yeah," Shelly said. "Tell that to Mick tomorrow. See ya'"

"Bye Shel" Jake returned the receiver to its cradle.

A County vehicle involved in a late night drug deal. The pieces of the puzzle were getting more bizarre all the time. Jake went to refill his empty coffee cup when the cordless phone started chirping.

"Hello."

"Jake…this is Billy. I'm on lunch break. I got some information for you." Billy Denton sounded out of breath.

"What'd you do run a marathon?" Jake replied. "You sound winded."

"I grabbed my sack lunch and ran to the pay phone down the street. I knew you'd want to hear what I found out as soon as possible."

"I appreciate the effort, Billy, but you didn't have to jog to the pay phone. Why not just call me from work?"

"Too risky." Billy spoke in a hushed tone of voice.

"Billy, are you being overly dramatic for a reason, or did you really find something?"

"Jake," Billy still spoke softly. "It's not what I found, it's what I didn't find."

"Really?" Jake said.

"Yeah," Billy continued. "I checked all five of the case files. There's no follow-up in any of them."

"What do you mean?"

"I mean the initial reports are in the files. The ones filled out by the first Deputy on the scene. But there's nothing after that. No interviews with friends or relatives…or neighbors; nothin' like that. And that stuff's always in there, I've seen it in other files. I like readin' that stuff. But it's not in any of those files. The only other reports in the file are the ballistics report and the report from the first Deputy on the scene. Let's see."

Jake heard the rustling of paper. "I made some notes…here it is. All the bullets were .22 caliber…all fired from the same weapon."

"So all the victims were killed by the same person…or at least the same gun," Jake responded. "But that's never come out in any media release."

"Yeah, I know," Billy said, "and that ain't all. All the cases were turned over to the same Detective. Detective Gerald Doogan. So Doogan's the one supposed to do the follow-up. Pretty weird just one Detective getting all those cases and not a one has any follow-up."

"What do you mean weird Billy?"

"Like…really strange. Most murder case files have tons of paperwork in them. These five have nothing. Almost like nobody cares."

"Maybe Detective Doogan is just swamped with work right now."

"Jake!" Billy said trying to show an air of confidence about his position. "These are murder cases…probably could be classified as serial murder cases…and nothing's been done on 'em. Doesn't make sense."

"Not much does right now. Is that all you've got?"

"Well, there is one more thing."

"What's that?" asked Jake.

"Four out of five of the crime scenes there were three sets of cowboy boot prints."

"The same cowboy boot prints at each scene?" asked Jake.

"Doesn't say," replied Billy. "Just says cowboy boot prints, and the victims were either wearin' tennis shoes or work boots, but not cowboy boots."

"So," Jake mused over the information trying to think of any questions that might have gone unasked. "The murder weapon is the same and the bad guys might wear cowboy boots. Sounds like somebody at the department must know that the murders are connected."

"Unless they're stupid," said Billy. "And they're not stupid around here."

"Okay...listen...thanks Billy. I really appreciate it. If you think of anything else, call, okay?"

"Sure, no problem, Jake"

"And Billy...I don't have to tell you, you gotta' keep this under your hat, okay?"

"Yeah, no problem Jake. I sure don't want to lose my job. Just don't tell nobody where you found this stuff out."

"My lips are sealed Billy. Talk to you soon." Jake hung up the phone.

"Same weapon, cowboy boots," Jake said to himself, and yet the Sheriff's Department's official statement to the press is "no suspects and no leads." But why no follow up investigation, and where in the heck does the mysterious County vehicle fit in? More pieces of the puzzle were falling into place. But the picture was still very porous. Maybe Jake could get a little professional advice tomorrow on the golf course from his friendly neighborhood Highway Patrol Officer.

CHAPTER 14

A Saturday morning golf game with CHP Officer Mick Williams meant one very important thing to Jake. Setting the alarm clock for 7 a.m. Mick was one of those guys who had to play golf early in the morning, so he didn't waste the whole day. Mick had to stay busy. He was twenty-nine years old and full of energy, or what Jake affectionately called "piss and vinegar." And on Saturday morning at 7 a.m. Jake hated "piss and vinegar."

The electronic rooster on his nightstand wasn't exactly rousting Jake from the best night's sleep he'd had in days. Jake's probing hand looked like a drunken tarantula crawling around as it finally located the offensive sounding clock, but in his attempt to tap the snooze button, Jake managed only to knock the small plastic timepiece on floor, where it continued it's monotonous buzzing. Stretching one arm as far as it would reach from underneath the covers, Jake finally got a grip on the annoying device. He quickly hit the "off" button and with all the energy he could muster, he tossed off the covers and drug himself out of bed, one leg at a time.

A short shower brought Jake somewhat out of his comatose state. He didn't shave however. He wasn't going to work, and he didn't have a date. Jake figured that, even if golf was a gentleman's game, it could be played just as nobly with stubble on your face. It would also be one less thing he would have to go through before he loaded up his golf clubs and headed to the course. Nuking a cup of instant coffee was even out of the question; too much time. Anyway, that's what god invented 7-eleven's for. Jake threw on a pair of Dockers, a golf shirt and a pair of flip-flops. He stuffed a pair of socks into his golf shoes, grabbed his golf clubs from the hall closet and headed out the door. Rick Rollins' Mustang was still parked in the driveway. Jake had called Rick the night before to say he'd be down to the Dog House sometime after his golf game to swap cars.

The Rosewood Golf Course was about 25 minutes from Jake's house. The city of Rosewood was a small farming community, but they didn't grow the typical valley crops. Galway Farms was famous worldwide for roses. The Galway family had been growing roses in the area since the early 1900's. In fact, Galway roses were internationally recognized, and often named for some of the most prominent world figures. Even half asleep, Jake loved the early morning drive out of suburbia. As the concrete and stucco of the city gave way to the irrigated fields of rural San Jacinto County, the fog always got a little heavier. Jake turned the heater up a notch and rolled down the window in the Mustang to savor the rich smell of soil, which seemed to be magnified by the moisture in the air.

Jake had his early morning golf routine down to a science. It took no more than forty-five minutes, from the unwelcome wail of the alarm clock to an empty Styrofoam cup being tossed in the trash at the golf course. And with a tee-off time of eight sharp, Jake had just enough time to say hi to Mick…take a few practice putts and head to the first tee. Jake never…ever…hit practice balls on the driving range. His simple philosophy was why waste your good shots, and your perfectly good energy, by taking strokes that don't count. At least that was the excuse Jake used over the years. It had become one of his golfing trademarks. People would quote him on occasion.

"Williams and Adams on the tee." The voice from the pro shop came over the public address. Jake made his way over to the first tee box. Mick was already there, limbering up his perfect swing that looked like a commercial for the PGA. Mick also dressed the part. Not only was he clean-shaven…he was dressed impeccably from head to toe, and Mick's entire ensemble was awash in some sweet smelling cologne.

"You're either taking this golf game way too seriously, or Shelly's dressing you," Jake joked. "Come clean Officer Williams.. which is it?"

"You know the old saying, Jake," Mick replied…"It's better to look good playing bad golf than it is to look bad playing good golf."

"Problem is," Jake said, rummaging around in his golf bag for a tee, "you do both…look good and play good, I mean."

Jake wasn't' joking with that remark. Mick Williams had a golf game to match his outfit. It was flawless. He actually played collegiate golf in Texas before moving to California. But since he was a much better golfer than Jake, Mick always had to spot Jake a few strokes…and Jake always took money from Mick like he was an ATM.

"Alright, Jake," Mick pointed to the tee box, "you wanna' go first?"

"Might as well put the pressure on early," replied Jake. He grabbed a ball out of his back pocket, a tee from his front and stabbed the two into the ground.

"You haven't hit one practice shot have you Jake?" Mick always tried to do his best to get the psychological advantage on Jake…but it didn't work.

"No I didn't," Jake calmly replied as he lined his Big Bertha up behind the golf ball. "I always like to save my best for first." Jake took a huge roundhouse swing at the dimpled orb and launched it far down the fairway…smack dab in the middle. "Now how would I feel if I'd have wasted that shot out on the driving range?"

Mick Williams could only laugh. He knew he would play a great round of golf…one just good enough to fall about twenty bucks short of Jake's.

* * *

Four hours and fifteen minutes later Mick's prediction was coming true. "Seven, eight, nine," Mick Williams slapped the last of the bills down on the small round Formica tabletop in the knotty-pine paneled clubhouse bar. "I had you down five bucks until the last three holes. How the heck do you do it?"

"The fine art of the press." Jake picked up the bills and tapped them into a neat pile. "Just when you think you have me where you want me, that's when just the opposite is true."

"But I beat you by ten shots today, Jake."

"But I beat you by two on the last three holes Officer Williams. I ask you, have you ever written a ticket to a speeder you haven't even pulled over yet?"

"I'm not sure I see the logic in that analogy, but I'm sure you do."

A petite waitress in jeans and a Rosewood tee shirt with a short boyish blond hairdo came over to set down a couple of longneck bottles of Bud.

"Would you like me to run a tab?" asked the pretty young waitress.

"No," replied Mick. "Just keep taking money from that pile of bills in front of Jake until they're all gone."

"Sure enough." She grabbed three of them, gave a cute smile and walked away. Soon there were two bottles of beer sitting in front of Jake and Mick.

"Okay," Mick began, "Bets are settled...beer's here...now back to this fantastic story you've been filling my ear with the last four hours."

Jake took a sip from the ice-cold bottle of beer. "Fantastic but true. It's all like some crazy dream...one I'm really not sure I like being involved in."

"You realize," Mick said, "that you could be making more out of this than it really is. I mean, let's look at the facts. You got some of your information from an admitted drug dealer, who was probably high on drugs when you talked to her, otherwise why in the world would she invite you over to her house in the middle of the night? You get told about a drug deal from a guy who's drinking beer and shooting pool in the afternoon at a known bad guy hangout. You got your inside information from a young man who isn't smart enough to even get through Criminal Justice in Junior College, and he's advising you on the status of an investigation into five murders. Not the most credible of witnesses I must say, Jake."

"You're right, Mick. But what about the drug deal? I saw it with my own two eyes."

"You saw what you thought was a drug deal...half awake at four in the morning. An unmarked county car...could have been doing anything...putting the sting on a fence for dealing in stolen goods...getting evidence from a confidential source...buying little league uniforms at discount rates. You didn't see drugs...you saw packages. Grandma's old china could have been in those boxes."

"Maybe you're right. It sure would ease my mind if you were right." Jake said. He took a much larger gulp from his bottle of Bud.

"But since we're on the subject of drug stories…let me share a little tale with you. And this is totally off the record, if you know what I mean."

"Sure, no problem," Jake replied.

Mick lifted the bottle of beer to his mouth and took a long pull. "This goes back probably five or six months…about the same time line as your dead drug dealers. We busted two vans and one station wagon…out on the Interstate. All Mexican nationals…all with large amounts of dope in the vehicle…mostly marijuana…some coke…some heroine. They were apparently headed here to the area somewhere. We get 'em in custody, but they don't stay long."

Mick stopped for a moment. Both men used the short pause in the conversation to wash down with the last of their beer. Jake held up his empty bottle toward the cute blonde waitress and held up two fingers. She gave a knowing nod and was quickly at the table with two fresh Budweiser's. She took three more dollars from the pile in front of Jake and went back to the bar.

Mick continued. "Three good drug busts…six suspects in custody. Now here's the rub. No prosecution. All the suspects have been released. Two allegedly back to Mexico to face charges there on a good neighbor law enforcement policy, or some such thing. Two more released for lack of evidence. Something about the vehicle being from a legitimate company and the suspects may not have known the drugs were in there to begin with. How bogus is that? And the other two escaped from a work detail while at the local holding facility."

"And this is all very unusual?" Jake asked.

"Unusual," Mick said in amazement. "I haven't seen that many suspects with a get out of jail free card since I been wearin' a badge. And Hord Matthews, the D-A is supposed to be one of the toughest in the State."

"He is," Jake replied. "I've seen the numbers. Matthews gets more jail time for more bad guys than any other county top cop around."

Mick took another pull at his longneck. "Our department's made inquiries. All we get is the old stonewall. What are we bustin' these guys for if they all wind up on the loose again?"

"I wonder," Jake interrupted, "if this could all be linked?"

"Oh yeah." Mick rolled his eyes. "It fits in very neatly. Problem is, it's a little far fetched. Dead drug dealers…County cars doing drug deals.…and the D-A's lettin' 'em go as quick as we can catch 'em…"

"All I know is that one of two things is true here," Jake said. "Either all of this points somewhere or it points nowhere…and I'm stuck right in the middle."

"I don't know what to tell you Jake. In my opinion without any hard evidence it doesn't amount to a hill of beans. And even if you had some, where are you going to go, the Attorney General?"

"Well," Jake lifted the Budweiser to his lips, "the next thing I'm going to do is ask a friend if he can find out anything about the drug busts that you say went sour."

Mick took a serious tone. "Just be careful Jake. If there is anything…anything at all to all of this circumstantial stuff, then there could be serious consequences to your getting real nosy around the wrong people."

"Yeah…I'll be careful, but I have to do it. I made a promise, and I may be savin' my own skin. Thanks for the game…and the beer. Oh and I'm leaving the rest of your money as a tip for little miss Budweiser. I'll talk to you soon." Jake got up...shook hands with Mick and headed out to Rick Rollins' Mustang. He needed to get the loaner back to his friend, and he needed another favor from his inside informant at the Sheriff's Department.

CHAPTER 15

Sunday morning found Jake standing in front of a place he hadn't been in quite a while, Eastside Evangelical. Jake figured if he was going to continue with this covert quest to get to the bottom of this story, he could certainly use a little help from above. Eastside Evangelical sounded like a good place to start asking for that help, and to make good on a promise to Mario Franklin.

The church wasn't your run of the mill place of worship, no fancy brickwork on the outside, no stained glass windows or wooden pews on the inside. Eastside Evangelical was a converted old supermarket in a half-empty strip mall in one of the poorest parts of East Butterfield. The grocery chain had abandoned the store years ago. Mario had taken out a lease on the vacant building. He mustered a small army of faithful with tool belts, gutted the place, laid down cheap carpet, erected a makeshift stage out of two-by-fours and plywood, and set up a few hundred folding chairs. Mario didn't believe in being ostentatious before the Lord, and God's word could be just as powerfully preached in an old supermarket as anywhere else. Salvation special on aisle number one.

The joyful noise of gospel singing, backed up by the crisp rhythm of a five piece band, could be heard a block away as Jake approached the double glass front doors. Church started at ten...the faithful began arriving at nine just to sing for an hour before the preaching even started.

"There's power in the blood of the Lamb" filled every corner of the makeshift sanctuary as Jake found a seat at the rear. A few of the faithful gave him a big smile...some a hearty handshake, but they kept on singing. Jake was handed several sheets of paper with the words to a number of hymns on them. He located the song being belted out by the brigade of worshipers and joined in.

From silk suits to scraggly tee shirts and tennis shoes, there was no dress code at Eastside. Jake's slacks and golf shirt would put him right in the middle of the clothing spectrum.

Hands were waving wildly in the air, and the amens were deafening as the final refrain of the hymn came to an end. The punctuation to the chorus was being fervently delivered by the drummer...a riff that also became the musical bridge to the entrance of Pastor Mario Franklin. Pastor Franklin walked up on stage with one hand in a praise salute in the air, the other holding a large black leather Bible. He was dressed in a black single-breasted suit, white shirt and red tie. He made no mention that Jake was in the audience, although it must have been very evident that he was there. "Mario was right the other day" Jake thought. He was the only white face in the crowd.

Mario launched into his sermon, one that couldn't have come at a better time with all the craziness that Jake had been going through lately..

Mario spoke eloquently and forcefully about how God never left your side. "I don't care how troubled things seem in your life," Mario reassured the congregation. "God is right there with you. And no matter what it is you're going through, there's nothing that God can't help you handle. That doesn't mean everything's going to be rosy. God's own son was tortured and sent to the cross. But it all worked out in the end. And it will all work out for you…if you just have faith."

That was exactly what Jake needed to hear. What he had to have most of all right now was faith. Faith that he was doing the right thing, faith that he wasn't going on some wild goose chase, and most of all, faith that it was all going to work out in the end.

Mario's high intensity exhortation wound down to the continued echo of amens from around the auditorium. Nearly an hour had gone by in what seemed like just a few minutes. Pastor Franklin led the crowd in an impassioned rendition of "Amazing Grace," then he gave his benediction to the crowd, confidently urging them to go in the peace and love of the Lord. He then walked to the back of the sanctuary to greet his flock as they left. Jake, being at the back of the auditorium, was one of the first to greet Mario.

"You're pretty good at this," Jake said as he met Mario with a hearty embrace.

"It's all the Lord's work," Mario replied with a broad smile. "I'm just the very fortunate vehicle the Lord has chosen to use. How's the investigation goin'?"

"Too good. I wish I had time to tell you."

"Call me next week and fill me in, and thanks for showin' up."

"To be honest with you Mario. I think you're sermon was just what the doctor ordered."

"It ain't the doctor Jake. It's the big physician in the sky. God bless you brother."

Jake gave Mario another hug and headed for the parking lot.

* * *

Thumbing through his address book at home, Jake felt a bit guilty calling his young friend Billy again. He didn't want to get him in any trouble or put him in harms way, but Jake didn't know anywhere else to turn. The weight of wanting answers was heavy on Jake's mind.

Jake found Billy Denton's cell phone number, tapped on his own phone's key pad and waited.

"Hello." Billy sounded like he had a mouth full of food when he answered the phone. Jake heard the loud voice of a sports commentator bellowing in the background.

"Billy, it's Jake."

"Jake…just a minute Jake let me turn down the t-v." Billy still sounded mush-mouthed. He hit the mute button on his remote control. The clamor of the t-v went silent. "There. What's up Jake?"

"I don't want to interrupt your football game, but I need to ask another favor."

"No problem…the 'Niners are gettin' killed anyway. Only game the Raiders are gonna' win all year, and it's against the Niners…go figure."

"I was just wondering if I can get you to check out a couple of things for me when you get back to work?"

"Sure, Jake, no problem. You must be hot on some story or somethin', huh?"

"Well, maybe. I'm not sure yet. Here's what I need help with. Three drug busts out on the Interstate in the last four or five months. All the suspects from Mexico…all with large amounts of marijuana and other drugs, and all busted by the

CHP. They were booked into the County Jail by the Sheriff's Department. Problem is, they were never prosecuted. Can you find anything out?"

"If we took custody of them from the CHP then we'll have a record, and it'll show what happened with the case. Tell you what I'll do Jake," Billy added, "I'll check it out today. I go in on the weekends every now and then and help 'em catch up on paperwork. If I find anything out I'll call you."

"Billy," Jake said. "Don't get in any trouble over this, okay?"

"Hey, Jake, they see me around there so much they won't think anything of it…don't worry!"

"Alright." Jake still felt uneasy asking Billy for the favor, but he did need the information. "Just be real careful."

"Not a problem…talk to you later Jake." And with that Billy hung up.

Rick Rollins' Mustang was still sitting out in his driveway, but the car swap would have to wait until later that evening. He kicked off his shoes…located the remote control on the coffee table, and hit the power button at the same time he let his entire body collapse into the well-padded sofa. The Forty Niners were still getting killed. He turned the volume down and immediately went to sleep.

CHAPTER 16

Billy waved to the guard at the security shack as he entered the parking lot at the back of the Sheriff's Department. The guard held up his hand, palm out, motioning for Billy to bring his Volkswagen Beetle to a halt.

The gray-haired security guard walked around to the driver's side of the car as Billy rolled down his window. "You sure you're paying attention to your calendar, Billy? This is Sunday afternoon."

"Yeah, Vern, just got a little tidyin' up to do at the office." Billy replied.

The guard laughed and shook his head…"Whatever they're payin' you, Billy, it ain't enough." He returned to his phone booth sized guard house, hit a red button on a console, and the large red metal arm swung upward, allowing Billy to enter the parking area.

The lot was nearly deserted, so Billy picked a parking spot near a heavy steel door that was at the rear entrance to the Sheriff's Department. The building housed the Sheriff's

Department offices and the County Jail, where inmates were booked and held. Billy exited the VW taking a small card from his pocket. As he approached the large metal door, he slid the card into a slot in a small black metal box that sat on a pedestal next to the door. A tiny red light went dark as a green light next to it started to blink, signaling Billy to enter. He grabbed the cold metal doorknob and turned it as he gave the bulky door a shove.

Just to the right was a small cubicle where the booking sergeant sat reading a magazine behind a bulletproof plate glass window with an opening about a foot square where the booking sergeant conducted his transactions over a metal countertop. Deputies and the bad guys they'd just arrested showed up here first. It was where the beginning of the booking process took place. The suspect's personal belongings were turned over to the booking sergeant, placed in a large manila envelope and filed away.

"Hey, Billy, what are you doing here on a Sunday afternoon?"

"Not much Sarge." Billy gave the sergeant a quick nod. "Just a little paperwork I want to catch up on before Monday morning rolls around. Besides the 'Niners are getting killed."

The sergeant shook his head. "You gotta' get a life, Billy." He went back to reading his magazine.

Billy walked to another large metal door which had a small glass and wire-mesh window, mostly used for those exiting the offices from the rear. You never knew what might be going on in the booking area. The sergeant pressed a button underneath his side of the countertop and a very loud buzzer sounded. Billy grabbed the metal doorknob, gave it a twist and headed down a long well lit hallway. Billy entered the second door on the right. The room was dark and dead quiet. With his right hand he felt around on the wall until he located the light switch. He gave it a flick and a bank of fluorescent lights came on overhead.

Even awash in light, the administration office took on eerie quality. It was as quiet as a tomb without the usual hubbub of activity. But it gave Billy a feeling of power and authority. With the office empty there was nobody to tell him what to do. It was the closest Billy ever got to being the law enforcement officer he always wished he could have become.

At the rear of the now brightly lit office was the door that led downstairs to the file room. The property room was also there. Billy didn't have access to the property room, which was where all of the confiscated weapons and drugs were kept. He opened the door; hit a switch on the wall at the top of the stairs and the entire area below filled with light. He stepped as lightly as possible down the metal stairs and headed to a bank of gray metal filing cabinets marked "TRANSFERS." The cavernous file room was as quiet as a mausoleum. He opened a file cabinet drawer and found the bright blue file divider marked CHP, and began thumbing through the folders. After pulling a few files that matched the dates he was looking for, the silence was shattered.

"Billy, what the hell are you doin' here?" the deep voice demanded.

Billy turned around. A chill suddenly grasped Billy's entire body. The man behind the voice was Detective Gerald Doogan, the detective whose name was on all the files of the dead men found in the fields outside of town, the detective who had done no investigation into any of the cases.

Billy had to swallow a couple of times before he found his voice. "Uh…just doin' a little filing." There was no way to hide the nervousness in his voice. "You know me…like to see everything caught up before Monday morning rolls around."

With a very unemotional look on his face, Detective Doogan took a slow, deliberate look around the file room as he put his hands on his hips, pulling back the sides of his suit coat, revealing a badge and a 9-millemeter Glock holstered on his belt.

Detective Doogan turned to Billy with a serious stone-jawed look. "But this is the transfer section, Billy. What in the world would you have to file in the transfer section?"

Billy felt like he'd been found out. "Oh, the transfer section." Billy turned to give the file cabinets a look, hoping to convince the Detective that he'd gone to the wrong area. "Must've made a mistake."

"Well, maybe I can help." Detective Doogan looked at the files Billy had removed and laid on top of the open cabinet. "Let's see what you got here."

"Oh, those are nothing," Billy felt the blood rushing out of his face, "just some files I found lying around in here."

"Oh really." Doogan didn't believe him. It was obvious.

Doogan took the files, gave them a look, and slowly raised his eyes to look at Billy. A slight grin crept up one side of his mouth. He shook his head and let out an audible exhale. "Very interesting Billy. Where'd you say you found these?"

"Uh…right here on the floor."

"Hmmm." the detective held the files in his right hand and slowly tapped them against the palm of his left. "For some reason Billy, I just don't believe you. It seems to me you're doing a little filing for the CHP…or maybe somebody else."

Detective Doogan returned the files to their proper place. He put his right hand on the Glock and his left hand firmly on Billy's shoulder. "I think it's time you and me had a little talk."

CHAPTER 17

Jake was still half-asleep has he drove the blue Mustang toward downtown Butterfield. He could have easily continued his nap on the sofa well into the night, but he'd kept Rick Rollins' Mustang long enough.

The sun had been down for about an hour, and as the evening air began to cool Jake could see the valley fog starting to settle back in. The streetlights were the first clue. They had begun to develop small moisture flecked halos around them. Several Harley-Davidson's were in the parking lot across the street from the Dog House as Jake pulled the Mustang in between the white lines. Stepping out of the car into the night air, the fog became even more noticeable. It quieted everything. It swallowed up sound and held the night in its clammy grip. Somewhere in downtown Butterfield steaks were being served at one of the local bistros. The scent of barbecue hung in the air; unable to escape the clutches of the stagnant mist that was rapidly enveloping the area. Jake didn't like the fog much. He disliked it even more now. It seemed to cast an eerie pall over his already perplexing predicament.

As Jake made his way towards the bar, the yellow light from a neon sign that spelled out "The Dog House" spilled down over the red brick exterior and poured onto the sidewalk, reflecting off the moisture that had begun to gather. As he got closer, Jake heard Bob Seger's gravelly voice coming from the jukebox inside…"Workin' on mysteries without any clues". 'Night Moves' was one of Jake's favorite Bob Seger songs, and it seemed to fit both the fog and his circumstances.

The smell of stale beer and cigarette smoke greeted Jake as he walked through the double swinging doors. Overhead two large round vents breathed warm air into the bar with a sound that had a mild asthmatic quality. Three men and three women, all in leather motorcycle garb shot pool in the back. They didn't even look up as Jake headed to the far end of the bar. Rick Rollins was on his usual perch with a newspaper in front of him. The paper was folded so that just the crossword puzzle was visible. Rick tapped the eraser end of the pencil on the bar without even looking up to acknowledge Jake's arrival.

"Six letter word for cow. Starts with B."

"How about 'bovine'" Jake threw his leg over a chrome legged bar stool with a red vinyl cover and put his feet on the bar rail.

"Works for me." Rick penciled in the word and looked up from the puzzle. "How's it hangin' Jake?"

"Not bad. Thought you might like your steed back."

"How's ol' blue been treating you?"

"Pretty good. Runs great. Just needs a coat of paint and I think you're off to the car show."

Rick laughed. "But if I get her painted, then the interior looks bad. If I get the interior fixed up, then the engine looks dirty. If I put chrome on the engine and get her all cleaned up, then I'm not gonna' want to drive 'er. So why not just leave 'er be?"

"That's what I love about you Rick, you're practical. Nothing too fancy about you."

"That's right buddy," Rick replied. "Practicality pays the bills and keeps the local barflies full of beer and wine. You're Jeep's down the street by the way. It's in that gated parking garage. I didn't want some stupid drunk taking a knife to those clear plastic windows of yours looking for spare change while that bright red thing was on my watch."

"Mighty thoughtful of you" replied Jake.

"So," Rick inquired, "how'd your secret mission go?"

"It went okay. Guess it's just as well ol' blue didn't have a new paint job. I might not have been as inconspicuous."

"Practicality pays again," said Rick. "So, we just swappin' keys or do you want a cold one."

"Sounds great," Jake replied. "It's starting to get foggy out there again. I knew the clear skies couldn't last that long around here."

Rick walked down to the middle of the bar. He grabbed a beer glass from a group of mugs sitting upside down on a piece of plastic mesh on top of the cooler, put it in a bin full of ice and gave it a few twists. He took the chilled mug, turned around to the three beer spigots behind him, tilted the glass and started to fill it with Budweiser.

As Rick walked back with the full mug of beer, the double doors to the bar swung open. A man in slicked-back dark hair and a dark gray single-breasted suit gave a small shiver and walked toward the center of the bar.

"Fog's back," said the stranger.

"Welcome to winter in the central valley," Rick deadpanned. "What'll you have?"

"Shot of tequila and a draft beer."

The stranger wore wire-rimmed glasses and smelled of forest scent cologne. He wore a white shirt and a red and blue striped tie. He could have been an insurance salesman or a lawyer. Whatever profession he was in, Jake thought; chances were his co-workers dressed pretty much the same.

"Here you go." Rick set the mug of beer down in front of the stranger. He grabbed a mixed drink glass and a bottle of Cuervo Gold from a lighted shelf under the glassware. He set the glass in front of the stranger and filled it with the gold liquid. "That'll be four fifty."

"Generous portions," the stranger said as he reached into his pocket, pulled out a few bills, peeled off a five and laid it on the bar.

"We aim to please," said Rick.

Rick walked down to the end of the bar and picked up a few empty beer boxes. "Jake, I'm gonna' just grab a couple of cases in the back real quick. Cover for me will ya'?"

"Sure, as long as the drink orders don't get too fancy," Jake replied.

Rick laughed as he headed to the stock room. "You're in The Dog House remember?"

The stranger took a sip of beer, tossed back the healthy shot of tequila, washed it down with a larger swallow of beer and turned to Jake. "You're the news guy aren't you?"

"Yeah," Jake said. "Jake Adams, Eyewitness News."

The stranger had an accountant's face and an emotionless voice. "You drive a red Jeep don't you?" The stranger took another large swallow from his glass of beer.

Curious, Jake thought. "Jeep Wrangler. My toy, or my mid-life crisis as some would call it."

The stranger finished off his mug of beer with one last gulp and turned to look at Jake. "Mister Adams. I've got this great story. I'd really like to get your thoughts on it…since you're in the business and all."

"Sure." How many times has this happened before, Jake thought. "Fire away."

"Can we go over to one of those booths there. It's kind of personal, if you know what I mean?"

"No problem. I guess I can keep an eye on Rick's bar from there."

"Thanks" said the stranger.

As they walked over to a corner booth, Jake could see the stranger looking around the bar, and at the bikers who still played pool in the back.

The stranger spoke almost in a whisper. "Mister Adams…may I call you Jake?"

"Sure," said Jake.

"Jake," the stranger continued "This story is about a guy who finds himself in the middle of a big mess." Jake could see the stranger was trying to pick his words very carefully. He continued in a very matter-of-fact tone of voice. "He pays a midnight visit to the widow of a drug dealer. She winds up dead."

Jake was shocked by the stranger's initial offering. His spine stiffened and a he felt a chill creeping over his body, but he kept quiet.

The stranger continued. "Somehow this guy finds out about a drug deal going down. He borrows a friend's blue Mustang so his bright red Jeep won't stand out, and he sees a lot of things he shouldn't see. Problem is, while the guy is asking a lot of questions, someone is watching. And, well Jake, the guy asking all the questions should be very nervous about the answers he's getting. Does this story sound familiar Jake?"

Jake's initial shock had settled. He was now simply amazed at what the stranger was saying. Being in the news business Jake was used to thinking quickly on his feet. He'd done it a million times live on the air when videotape or reporter packages didn't roll, or live reports from the field suddenly turned to snow. Now the coolness under pressure he'd learned over the years came quickly into play. Jake was admittedly nervous, but he wasn't afraid.

"It sounds vaguely familiar," Jake said without missing a beat. "Is this the plot of some mystery novel or something?"

"I'm glad to see you've kept your sense of humor through all of this Jake. It's that sense of humor that we all love so much about you."

"Who is 'we all'?"

"Jake," the stranger stared unblinkingly. "We are the ones who don't want to see you hurt, possibly even killed over all of this nonsense."

"I didn't realize that was an option," Jake responded. "I'm afraid I'm just following my journalistic instincts."

"Then your instincts should tell you when you're getting too close to something that's a lot bigger than you can handle." The stranger's serious expression and tone of voice didn't change.

"Obviously, you know a lot," Jake said. "But I'm not exactly sure how to take all of this."

The stranger stood up. A curious look came over his face, as if surprised that Jake was so even tempered through the past few moments.

"You should take it…very seriously, Mister Adams. Thank you for listening to my story." The stranger turned and walked out through the double swinging doors and into the night.

Jake's next move came swiftly. He moved quickly to the far end of the bar where a small door led to the stock room, and eventually to another door that opened up on the alley. Jake met Rick who was pushing a dolly loaded with cases of beer.

"Be right back," Jake said as he moved hastily past Rick toward the back door.

"Front door broken?" Rick yelled. But Jake was gone.

Jake splashed through small puddles of water and past large rubber trash containers that smelled of stale booze and rotting food. He made his way to the end of the red brick building, and stopped. Slowly moving his head past the edge of the brick, Jake peered around the corner. The street was empty, but through the quiet of the night Jake heard the muffled sound of a car door closing somewhere down the street. Jake followed the noise, sprinting down half a block before he heard an engine start up. He ducked into the doorway of a darkened vacuum cleaner shop and waited. The sound of a car kicking into gear forced Jake's head out into the open again. In the middle of the next block, Jake saw taillights pull out of a parking spot and head down the street away from him. The exhaust created a plume of steam as it met the cold damp air. Making out a license plate number was impossible, but the type of car was obvious as it entered the street. It was a large white Chevy sedan.

He watched as the taillights disappeared into the night. A moment later he walked back through the double swinging doors of The Dog House.

"In quite a hurry there, Jake," Rick said as Jake came back in the bar. "And out the back door yet. Mighty mysterious stuff going on here."

"Oh, you have no idea," Jake replied.

"Don't suppose you'd like to tell ol' Rick about it?"

"If I told you," Jake said and let the sentence hang in the air.

"Yeah, I know," said Rick. "You'd have to kill me. Right?"

"You got it buddy."

Rick walked over to where the stranger's empty shot glass and beer mug sat. He grabbed a small towel, began wiping down the bar, and turned to Jake.

"Son-of-a-buck," Rick muttered, "the guy didn't even leave a tip."

Jake looked at Rick and shook his head. "Oh, I wouldn't be so sure about that."

CHAPTER 18

Jake took a bite of refried beans as he sat on the patio outside Garcia's Mexican Restaurant. Garcia's was owned by an affable Hispanic fellow name Manuel. Jake had gone to the establishment for years. It was one of the few eateries that Jake returned to over and over. The food was good and Manuel always treated Jake like family. He'd chosen the patio for lunch even though the ubiquitous haze put a chill in the air. Jake wanted to keep his head as clear as possible.

The fog wasn't thick, but it hung there like a stubborn shroud. The cars and pedestrians moved through the mist in Jake's field of vision reminding him of the grainy quality of an old moviola he'd seen in a nickel machine at the county fair when he was a youngster.

As Jake saw it, he had two simple options, continue to snoop around or drop the whole thing like a hot potato. Whatever information Billy Denton might offer up could help make up his mind. Jake would see what Billy had to say, and then he'd make a decision. Even with all that had happened, fearing for his own life still wasn't part of the equation, even after the intimidating stranger had issued a fairly stern warning. Jake was sure the stranger felt a warning would be enough to curtail his investigative adventure. The stranger was wrong of course. But just to be on the safe side, Jake had rummaged through his sock drawer the night before to locate his .38 revolver. The .38 spent that night under Jake's pillow.

Jake took a few bites of the enchiladas and then spent the rest of his time moving the rice and beans around the plate with his fork.

"You're not very hungry today," Manuel startled Jake, suddenly appearing at the table.

"No," Jake replied. "My eyes were bigger than my stomach as my Grandma used to say."

"Doggie bag?" Manuel asked.

"Sure. Thanks Manuel." The Hispanic man turned and walked back into the restaurant.

* * *

At home Jake put the Styrofoam container in the refrigerator. The food would never see the inside of the microwave. Jake loved cold leftovers. To Jake, most food was better cold than hot. Whenever he'd order pizza, he'd grab one piece and put the rest in the fridge to let it chill. Eating cold food was a habit he'd learned as a young boy visiting his Grandparents in rural Alabama.

Some of Jake's fondest memories harkened back to his days as a pre-teen visiting his Mother's parents. They were farmers. The closest paved road was miles away from the small farmhouse where his Mother was raised. Jake was raised in Dallas, and after Jake's mother and father divorced; he and his mom took regular summer treks to rural Alabama. In his first few visits they would stay a couple of weeks. As Jake grew older, he would take the bus to stay much of the summer with his grandparents. He loved the country. It became part of him. Love of the outdoors was something that was still with Jake, having much to do with his frequent trips to the local countryside in his Jeep.

Jake was nine years old the first time he and his Mom made the daylong drive just across the Mississippi line. It was, to say the least, a bit of a culture shock for young Jake. His grandparents didn't even have an outhouse. Going to the bathroom meant walking down a dirt path toward a large stand of corn and veering off the path into the pine trees, with a roll of toilet paper in hand. That was only one inconvenience. There was no television. A small radio was the only over-the-airwaves entertainment. Jake however, found that he quickly warmed to the rural lifestyle, and within a short time he embraced it. Jake's proudest moment came when his young bare feet could handle running down the gravel and dirt road where his cousins played. He felt as if he'd passed some sort of initiation. He felt as if he was finally, and truly, a country boy. That feeling of being a country boy never left Jake.

Jake had fond memories of the things like going to a creek and fetching buckets of water so cold it made your teeth chatter to drink it. And the water wasn't the only cold thing that Jake learned to appreciate.

The big meal of the day at his grandparents' house was "dinner", and it was served at midday. The word "lunch" wasn't in their vocabulary. And everything they ate came from what they grew. Black-eyed peas and cornbread, sweet corn and fried okra, were the mealtime staples in the small farmhouse. Grandma was a great cook, and his earliest memories were of her living in the kitchen. To this day, the smell of okra frying and cornbread cooking were a vivid part of Jake's childhood recollections, along with other memories like home-churned butter and home-made ice cream. Even Lurene's Diner, on its best nights couldn't come close to Grandma's home cooking.

What the brood of aunts and uncles and nieces and nephews didn't eat during dinner, Grandma covered with a red and white checkered cloth and put up in the cupboard until the evening meal. "Supper" as country folk called it was served right around dusk, when everyone came in from the days work…and it was served just the way it came out of the cupboard…at room temperature.

Grandma took the large bowls and platters full of leftovers down from the cupboard, removed the checkered cloth, and everyone waded in. At first, Jake thought the evening meal tradition was a bit odd. But once he developed a taste for the un-warmed food, it became his favorite meal. He would fill his plate with the leftover black-eyed peas, sweet corn, and fried okra, and mix them all together into a culinary concoction that would never be equaled the rest of his life.

Jake had even tried buying the main ingredients at the store in a feeble attempt at re-creating from a can what Grandma had taken all day to prepare. It was useless. There was something magical Grandma did to the food. A secret ingredient she took with her to the grave.

Those were the good old days, Jake thought. Nine years old and running barefoot down an old dirt road with his cousins, the smell of red clay and pine trees in his nostrils. Jake had thought about moving there years ago after his divorce. But it was just a nostalgic notion. Besides, Jake thought, Butterfield and the adjacent mountains and countryside were a pretty good substitute for those youthful days down on the farm.

Jake's childhood flashback ended as he shut the refrigerator door and noticed the blinking red light on his answering machine. He pushed the play button and after a couple of beeps he heard the voice of the Assignment Editor, Ed Olson. "Jake, this is Ed. Give me a call at the station as soon as you can. It's pretty important."

There was a sense of urgency in Ed's voice. Jake had been called from work before for a variety of reasons, but Ed's voice sounded different this time. Jake grabbed the handset from its cradle on the kitchen counter and punched in the newsroom number.

"Eyewitness News." Ed Olson's voice came on the line.

"Ed, this is Jake. What's up?"

"Bad news Jake. You're friend Billy, he's dead."

It took a second for the news to sink in. When it did, Jake felt the strength drain from his body. If the kitchen counter weren't there for him to lean on, Jake would have collapsed in a heap on the floor.

"Billy's dead?" Jake heard a hollow ringing in his ears as he uttered the words. "What...uh.. what happened?"

"He drowned. Sheriff's Department found him in his car in a canal this morning. He apparently ran off the road sometime late last night. They say they found a bunch of empty beer cans in the car."

Jake was in shock. This was no accident, he thought. Something happened while he was looking through files for Jake. He felt awful...no he felt empty...like he'd murdered his own friend. "What uh...what else do we know, anything?"

"That's about it," Ed answered. "Except we didn't actually hear about it on the scanner."

"What do you mean?"

"Well, the Sheriff's Department knew how close you were to Billy. So a Detective Doogan called this morning to tell us that he'd been found in the canal."

"Doogan," Jake blurted out the name. Doogan was the Detective Billy had said took over the five murder cases. Doogan was the Detective that did no follow up on any of those cases, and now Doogan was calling the t-v station to personally let Jake know that his friend Billy was dead. Detective Doogan was tied to Billy's death somehow, Jake could sense it. Blaming any of this craziness on coincidence now was out of the question.

Jake was silent for a moment. "Uhh…I'm probably Billy's closest friend. I'll call the department and see if there's anything I can do."

"I guess so," replied the assignment editor. "I don't know what you can do. Everybody here's just beside themselves about this. You gonna' be okay?"

"Yeah, I'll be alright. Let me talk to the boss, okay?"

"Sure, Jake. Just a minute."

The News Director, Loren Christopher came on the line. "Jake, I don't know what to say. I'm terribly sorry. How are you holding up?"

"I'm not sure Loren. I'm pretty numb right now," Jake said. "I think I'll take a few days off if it's okay with you."

"No problem, Jake. Take all the time you need. I know he was like family to you."

"Thanks, Loren. I'll check back in a few days."

"Sure Jake. If you need anything don't be afraid to call."

"Thanks." Jake hung up the phone. He thought of the News Director's last words, "don't be afraid." That unfortunately was exactly what Jake was at present. It was an emotion he wasn't used to. And even with all that had gone on the past few days, it was an emotion that hadn't entered the picture in full force…not until now.

Jake grabbed his small telephone directory and looked up

the Sheriff's Department number. He punched in the numbers and waited. A very businesslike voice came on the line, "Sheriff's Department."

"Detective Doogan, please" Jake said.

He wasn't sure this was a good idea, but then Jake wasn't sure of anything right now.

"Detective Doogan's office" a friendly young voice came on the line.

"Hi, this is Jake Adams. Is Detective Doogan in?"

"Mister Adams," the young voice responded with shocked sympathy. "I'm so sorry to hear about Billy. Everybody around here just loved him. I know how close you were to Billy. He talked about you all the time."

"Thank you," Jake said. "That's very kind of you. Yes, we were very close. I understand Detective Doogan called to notify me at work this morning. Is he around?"

"Yes, Mister Adams, he's on the phone right now, but I'll put you through as soon as he's off."

"Thank you," Jake said.

Jake wasn't sure exactly how he was going to handle this conversation. His years of on-air experience wouldn't allow him to show too much emotion. Instead of letting his anger take over, Jake would act as normal as possible, letting the conversation take its course.

A deep gravelly voice, probably from years of interrogating suspects in smoke filled back rooms Jake thought, came on the line. "Mister Adams. I'm sorry to be the one to bring you the bad news about your friend."

Jake kept his questions short and to the point. "Detective Doogan…uh thanks for calling earlier today, but I have to know, how did Billy die?"

"Why, from drowning, Mister Adams. Apparently Billy had

been drinking and went for a late night ride. We found several beer cans in the car. There were no skid marks. It looks like he just ran off the road."

"Detective Doogan," Jake was trying his best not to take an accusatory tone. "Billy and I were close friends. I was probably the only close friend Billy had."

"That's what I understand," said the detective. "That's what makes this such a hard job sometimes."

"But since I knew Billy so well, there are a couple of things that puzzle me."

"What would that be?" The sympathetic tone was gone from Detective Doogan's voice. He now sounded much more professional.

Jake got right to the point. "Billy didn't drink that much. I mean, one beer was about his limit. So I can't understand why there were so many beer cans in the car. If he drank more than one he wouldn't have been able to make it out of the driveway."

"Well, Mister Adams," the slightest hint of defensiveness began to creep into the detective's voice. "He may have consumed the alcohol somewhere near the canal, then accidentally drove into the canal trying to navigate his way home."

"Possibly," Jake paused, ready to make his final point to the gruff and serious sounding detective. "But Billy couldn't drive at night. He had awful night vision. Even the thought of driving after dark scared him. In fact, there've been a number of occasions when I've picked him up at work at the Sheriff's Department when he had to work late. Just ask any of the people in the administrative section. Driving at night would have been completely against the grain for Billy."

"Mister Adams," the detective was calm and very matter-of-fact. "I'm not in the business of assessing the state of mind of an accident victim. I'll leave that to the psychologists. It could be a simple case of a mistake in judgment. I see it my line of work all the time." He paused…"Some people just make bad decisions sometimes Mister Adams, and they suffer the consequences…if you know what I mean."

Detective Doogan's last words were deliberate, Jake thought, possibly meant to send a message to Jake. And at present, regardless of all the emotions running through Jake's mind, he had no recourse but to acknowledge the detective's rationale.

"Yes, I suppose your right," said Jake. "We all suffer the consequences of our decisions. Thanks for you time."

"Your quite welcome, and I'm very sorry about your friend." Detective Doogan hung up the phone.

Jake was still leaning against the kitchen countertop as the phone call ended. He held the receiver at arms length, staring at what he believed was his momentary connection with someone who knew very well how Billy Denton died. After returning the handset to its cradle, Jake walked back to the bedroom. He grabbed the .38 from beneath his pillow and walked back out to the living room. His legs felt like a load of sandbags as he sat on the couch and put his feet up on the coffee table. The revolver dropped into his lap as his head fell back into the sofa. Jakes eyelids felt heavy, but sleep was something that would be impossible. His body was dog tired, but his mind was racing, trying to decide his next move.

One piece of evidence in his possession was still unconnected. That would be Jake's next step, and then he would need a safe place to put the puzzle together. That decision was easy. But for right now it was time to put his sorrow over Billy Denton's death on hold. It was time to head downtown.

CHAPTER 19

Seated in his high backed leather chair, he tapped his pen repeatedly on the top of the large oak desk. It was the only sound in the room as he looked at the other two men who were seated directly across from him. He was the man in charge, and the other two men were waiting for his decision on what to do next. Finally, he spoke.

"Our Mister Adams is proving to be quite a nuisance. I'm afraid he may know far too much. And he is, after all, a newsman, a very popular newsman. This story could wind on the evening news, and we could all wind up in prison. The problem facing us now is, of course, what to do with him."

"For god's sake," said the more nervous of the other two men. "We're talking about Jake Adams here. People love this guy. If something happens to him, the spotlight may get really bright, and it may burn all of us."

The third man spoke up. "But it's a fact…Jake Adams put Billy up to looking through files that directly connect us, not only to the murders, but also to the drug runners that never went to trial. He knows, or at least suspects, far too much. Something has to be done. We've come this far. I say we go all the way. We've got to cover our tracks completely. If we're going down for seven murders, why not go down for eight?"

"But who else has he talked to about what he knows?" the nervous man chimed in. "Are we going to kill everyone who Jake may have come in contact with?"

The man behind the desk stood up and walked over to the ceiling-to-floor window and put his hands in his pockets. "Gentlemen. Here's exactly what we will do." He turned around to face the two men who waited on his decision. "We will do what is necessary. We will take care of business. And right now our business is taking care of Jake Adams."

CHAPTER 20

The digital clock in Jake's Jeep said 4:08 as he looked for a parking spot just off Jefferson Avenue. The downtown area was busy in the late afternoon rush to get the days business done. Just over an hour away from setting, the winter sun looked like a small fuzzy orange in the fog filled sky as it made its final descent into the western horizon. People in business suits stood on curbs and looked for an opening in the traffic before darting across the street with their arms full of files and folders. UPS and Federal Express vans were double parked as their uniformed drivers scurried in and out of local shops. The streets were full of cars; some doing last minute business, some getting an early start on their evening. And all of this hustle and bustle suited Jake just fine. Blending into the crowd was exactly what he had in mind. His business would take no more than ten or fifteen minutes. If he found what he was looking for he would be in and out like a flash.

Right now though Jake's main concern was finding a discreet place to park his bright red Jeep. He didn't know who, if anyone, would take note of his presence, but at this stage of the game Jake didn't want to take any chances.

Driving down 24th Street, one block north and parallel to Jefferson Avenue, Jake saw exactly the location he needed. The old First Christian Church complex would fit his purposes just fine. There were a number of cars already in the lot adjacent to the large brown sandstone building, which had been in downtown Butterfield since the early 1950s. First Christian was much more than just a place of worship. For years it had been a meeting place for all sorts of local organizations involved in efforts to help the needs of the community. Jake found a parking place in between a full sized van and a large sport utility vehicle. He pulled in and shut off the engine.

With his jeans, pullover golf sweater, and Dodger's baseball cap, Jake was sure he wouldn't be recognized. Just to make sure he remained anonymous he put on a pair of wrap-around sunglasses, cheap knockoffs of the Oakley variety. He locked the Jeep and headed for Jefferson Avenue and the County Courthouse.

Jake had been in the Courthouse on a number of occasions, both professionally and personally. Most recently his visit to the large glass and stucco structure was in response to a jury summons. Jake received a notice to perform his civic duty every couple of years. County officials assured him that the jury pool was selected at random, mostly from DMV and registered voter records, but Jake thought differently. If jury pool names were chosen in lottery fashion, then why was his called on such a regular basis? Jake didn't care really. In fact, he rather enjoyed the judicial process. Six times he'd been called to jury duty. Four of those times he'd actually been selected as a juror. Conventional wisdom in the news business was that if you were a journalist you would be excused as a juror because both the prosecution and the defense thought you had too much prior knowledge about the case being tried. That myth was quickly laid to rest. Jake discovered that his honest face and his honest answers to the presiding judge's questions made him the perfect candidate to evaluate evidence given on the witness stand. So, after having served on four juries, his familiarity with the County Courthouse was about to give Jake an edge in trying to complete a very necessary task in his search for the truth.

Crossing Jefferson Avenue at the light, Jake headed for the large glass double-doors that led inside the spacious lobby of the Courthouse. A large round fountain bubbled away in the middle of the plant filled atrium. But before you ever set foot on the blue and gold tiled floor you had to pass through a security checkpoint. Uniformed guards stood watch as Jake walked through the metal detector, tossing his keys into a tray held by a female guard.

Neither of the sentinels seemed to recognize Jake as he walked through the electronic gateway. Grabbing his keys from the plastic tray, Jake headed to the right where an escalator carried people to and from the second floor, which housed all of the county courtrooms. A flood of dull gray light from a wide bank of windows filled the upper floor as Jake made the short ride up the stepped conveyor. Once on the second floor Jake found himself facing a long hallway with the windows on one side and solid oak double doors that opened into half a dozen courtrooms on the other. The frontage hall was empty. Four o'clock in the afternoon was the end of the day for most juries, and most judges like to give their panelists a good nights sleep and an evening with the family before resuming their duties the next day. Besides, most judges, attorneys, and clerks had their hands full of paperwork well after four in the afternoon.

Apparently all the juries that were hearing cases had gone home for the day as Jake scanned the hallway. At the end of the corridor, Jake's eyes zeroed in on a single door with stenciled white letters that read "Jurors Only." Jake had been through that door numerous times, and that's where he was headed now. Whenever a juror was not required to be in the courtroom listening to evidence or instructions from the judge, they were welcome to take advantage of the juror's break room. The break room had vending machines that dispensed everything from fresh fruit to deli sandwiches, from soda to coffee. You could grab a snack and relax at any one of a number of round Formica tables or vinyl-covered booths. And all of these in-house comforts were serenaded by a very benign blend of piped in music.

But it wasn't the amenities that drew Jake to the second floor of the County Courthouse building today. In the back of the "break room" were three doors. Two of the doors had blue plastic signs on them, one reading "Women", the other "Men". In between the two was a single door with black-stenciled letters, which read "Parking". That was where Jake's eyes were now focused.

Once you were selected to serve as a juror, you were allowed to use the underground parking garage. Space permitting, this enabled jurors to enter and exit the courthouse without the hassle of trying to find a parking place somewhere downtown. Getting into the underground garage from the street required driving past another security guard and showing him your "JUROR" badge. Entering the garage from the juror's break room eliminated that. And the parking area was crucial to Jake for one very important reason…the county owned vehicles also parked there.

Moving quickly down the zigzag set of stairs Jake passed the door that read "Lobby" and continued down the stairs until he reached another large metal door which said "Garage." Jake grabbed the stainless steel doorknob and gave it a twist. The cold and cavernous expanse of the parking garage was a stark change from the fluorescent glow of the Courthouse. As Jake's eyes adjusted to the sparsely lit parking area, he noticed the shapes a few people walking in the distance. He heard the echoed sounds of car doors slamming, and the muffled growl of engines coming to life. Other than those few people departing the building, the garage was empty.

To his immediate right was the section of parking spaces reserved for the people who worked in the building. Most of the cars were privately owned. But some were county vehicles, driven by county officials. Some would have the telltale 'EXEMPT' on the top of the license plate, which indicated that it was "exempt" from state fees. Other county plates would look like any other license plate. It was this type of plate that Jake hoped to find.

A large white Chevy sedan was half of what Jake was looking for, the other half of the equation was on the small piece of paper in his pocket...a number that Jake now had memorized...1SUB727.

As Jake walked to his right, a long line of parked cars led to an elevator about 200 feet away. Late model Chevy and Ford sedans, mostly white or tan, some with an "EXEMPT", some without, were parked along the row, but none with the winning numbers Jake was looking for. As he neared the elevator some of the parking spaces had white lettering stenciled on the concrete wall at the front of the parking space with titles like "County Commissioner" and "County Assessor." Still, none of the plates contained the sequence of letters and numbers that would complete Jake's search.

Jake reached the double door elevator. It was the type that had no buttons, only a slot to insert a key card. This private conveyor took its occupants to floors that the general public was not allowed to visit, at least from this vantage point. On the other side of the elevator there were only three more parking spaces, and then a concrete wall with an arrow pointing to the left and the word "EXIT." Only one of the three spaces was occupied. The lone car was a large white late model Chevy sedan.

As he approached the rear of the car Jake wasn't holding out hope of finding what he was looking for, but as the numbers on the license plate came into view, it was like watching your winning lottery numbers rolling across the television screen. It was a jackpot in off-white with blue lettering..."1SUB727." Jake's eyes moved quickly from the license plate to the concrete wall that formed the headstone of the parking space. Jake just stared. It was the proverbial and symbolic, yet very literal, 'writing on the wall.' Yet of all the emotions that marched through Jake's senses, fear wasn't one of them. He actually felt relieved. Stenciled in white just above the hood of the Chevy sedan were the words, "Butterfield City Mayor."

It was a huge piece of this bizarre puzzle. A few smaller pieces were yet to be fitted into this crazy jigsaw journey, but now the picture was oh so much clearer. An old Butterfield saying thrust its way into Jake's thoughts..."The Three Amigos." Jake now knew what he might be up against. It was time to make a phone call.

CHAPTER 21

As Jake made his way back to the First Christian Church parking lot, he pulled his cell phone out of his jacket pock, punched in seven numbers and hit send. After a couple of rings a feminine voice that reminded Jake of Lauren Bacall came on the line, "Hello."

"Maddy...it's Jake. What's up?"

"Well I'll be darned...my horoscope said a tall dark handsome man would come into my life today. Guess I'll have to settle for a tall gray haired one."

"Remember," Jake shot back, "gray means older, and older means more experienced."

"Define experience."

"I'd love to but I'm in a church parking lot right now, and it's cold."

"Well, why don't you just come on over and let me warm you up?"

"Actually, Maddy, that's exactly what I had in mind. Except it's a little more than that. I don't want to sound like I'm coming over on business or anything, but could I park my Jeep in your garage?"

"Is that some sort of sexual innuendo or something?"

Jake laughed. "No, I'm serious. I don't want my Jeep to be seen there."

"Has my reputation gotten that bad?"

"You're reputation is in great shape. It's just that mine isn't doing so great right now...within a certain circle of people. I'll explain when I get there, I promise."

"Alright Mister Mysterious News Guy. Tell you what I'll do. I'll put the garage door opener in the mailbox by the driveway. You just pull in the garage and come on in. And.. oh yeah...make sure you're not followed."

"When I get there, please remember that last sarcastic remark of yours. See you in a bit"

Jake had arrived at his Jeep. He folded the cell phone...reached in his pocket for his keys...unlocked the Jeep door and climbed in, depositing the folded phone in a cup holder in the center console.

Maddy was only joking, but Jake did make sure he wasn't followed. He began with what would be a regular series of checks of his rearview mirror as he left downtown. It was, Jake thought, a necessary precaution considering his present circumstance. The last thing Jake wanted was to get Maddy involved in all of this. But he figured...Maddy's house was a good place to hide out and gather his thoughts. Maddy could also have her own inspirational input into the mire of facts that he had to sort through. But most importantly Jake thought, just being near this warm and beautiful woman for a while would cure a plethora of pains.

Sandcastle Lane was in an upscale neighborhood just west of town. Jake didn't drive straight there. He took just enough side streets to ensure that he was the only one heading to Maddy's house...*serpentine* was the word that came to mind...a reference to an old Alan Arkin/Peter Falk movie called *The In-Laws*. The sun was down and the fog had settled in for the night as Jake pulled into Maddy's driveway. He rolled the window down as he approached Maddy's mailbox, which sat perched atop a white post adjacent to the driveway. Jake reached out and opened the mailbox. Inside was the small plastic box with a white button on it. He punched the white button with his thumb and the sectional garage door began to open. He pulled in and tapped the garage door opener again. As the garage door clattered shut, the door leading into the house opened. There stood a tall slender feminine figure. As the garage door made its final trek down the metal runners, Jake let out a sigh of relief. The simple sound of the garage door closing seemed to separate him from all of the tensions and worries on the other side.

Fatigue had started to settle into every joint in Jake's body as he climbed out of the Jeep and made his way to the open doorway and Maddy's open arms. The door closed behind them as the two hugged quietly for a moment. Maddy was still damp from a recent shower. The rain-fresh aroma of shampoo mixed with the sweet smell of powder and perfume filled Jake's nostrils. Maddy had readied herself quickly for Jake's impromptu arrival. She wore a light blue terry cloth robe, and with her moist brunette hair pinned up on the top of her head, Jake softly kissed her neck as he held her in a secure embrace.

Jake had known Madeline Scofield for over ten years. They'd met at a United Way fundraiser. Madeline's husband was being honored that night for his work with the needy, both in the Butterfield area, and in a number of small towns in Mexico. Jake served as the emcee for the black tie affair.

Dr. Benjamin Scofield was a well-respected ophthalmologist. After years of operating a very successful eye clinic locally, Dr. Scofield started donating his talents to those in the community who would never have been able to afford eye care on their own. But eye care for the local needy wasn't enough for Benjamin Scofield. He enlisted the help of some his medical golfing buddies, and soon the Scofield Clinic was opened in East Butterfield. The Clinic was a godsend for the area, and received rave reviews in medical journals all over the country. But the team of physicians didn't stop there.

Just over a year after the clinic opened, Dr. Scofield decided his medical crew should take their talents south of the border into Mexico. It was a decision that was influenced by the large numbers of Hispanics who came into the East Butterfield clinic, many of whom mentioned relatives in some of the impoverished areas of rural Mexico, wishing they could get the same treatment. It wasn't long before the medical team loaded a private jet with supplies, and with the blessing of the Mexican government, headed down to do what would seem like a miracle to the poorest of the poor. Jake had followed the progress and the itinerary of Dr. Scofield's medical expeditions, both in news coverage, and as a passenger on one of the team's trips to Mexico. What began as a journalistic desire to cover this philanthropic physician's venture into uncharted medical territory, turned out to be an enduring relationship with the Scofield family. At a time when Jake was going through a tough separation from his wife, it seemed as if the Scofield family was adopting him. He spent endless hours with Maddie and Ben. Sometimes it was dinner at their spacious abode, other times it was Jake who took the Scofield's to a remote mountain retreat that he had discovered in his Jeep. It was actually the first time outside of his own shaky marriage that Jake felt like he'd found family.

Jake had been part of the Scofield family for several years when tragedy struck. On a solo trip to Mexico in his own small plane, to scout out the medical team's next adventure, Benjamin Scofield died in a fiery crash. The medical community and scores of others who knew of Dr. Scofield's desire to help the needy, were hard pressed to come to grips with the death of such a giving and generous person. But Ben's wife Maddy came apart at the seams.

Maddy was by no means just the wife of a world-renowned doctor. She was well respected in her own right in Butterfield. As an attorney, and part of the hard nosed District Attorney's Office, Madeline Scofield had helped put away some of the most notorious characters who ever surfaced on the streets of Butterfield. Her legal prowess was unparalleled. But when her husband died, a large part of Maddy died as well.

Throughout this entire dark episode in Maddy's life, the only saving grace was the very simple fact that Jake Adams was at her side. No one else seemed to comfort Maddy like Jake. Whenever Maddy needed a shoulder to cry on or someone to talk to, the only person she really felt comfortable with was Jake. And about the time that many in the community wondered if Maddy would ever pull out of her depression, it was Jake who made the simplest of suggestions that turned Maddy's life around.

It was another night when Maddy sat silently on the sofa, listening to old Frank Sinatra records, that Jake made the suggestion that put Madeline Scofield back on the road to recovery.

"Maddy," Jake said, "why don't you find a way to continue doing what Ben was doing? Not in the operating room, but in the courtroom."

It was as if a light had been turned on in the darkest of rooms. Maddy looked at Jake that night and smiled, the first smile Jake had seen on her face in some time. It was that night that Maddy decided to give up the District Attorney's Office and start practicing law for the people on the other side of the fence, the people who would never be able to afford a good lawyer. It was that night that the seeds of the Scofield Legal Defense Council were born, started by Maddy, but dedicated to her late husband Ben.

Six months later Maddy had a team of attorneys on board, helping the needy with a wide range of legal matters, and at a special dinner at the Red Lion Inn, Maddy acknowledged all the help she'd received putting the organization together. At the top of the list of accolades Maddy handed out while standing at an oak podium in front of hundreds of attorneys and benefactors, Maddy said a sincere thanks to Jake Adams, "without whose support through tough times, and who's clear thinking through my own cloud of depression, I might never have climbed out of the abyss."

A big smile filled Jake's face as Maddy turned to face him at the end of her complimentary remarks. Jake had known a number of women in his life. He wasn't sure that any had meant as much to him, in so many ways, as Madeline Scofield.

Jake drove Maddy home that night. They shared a bottle of chilled white wine while they sat on the off-white velour sofa in Maddy's living room. They shared memories of the things the three of them had done when Ben was alive. The stories lasted well into the second bottle of wine. At two in the morning, when the last glass was empty, Jake smiled at Maddy and said.. "I've either got to go or crash on your couch."

Maddy returned Jake's infectious smile and tossed her head back in school-girl fashion. She pulled her shoulder length brunette hair back with both hands and looked at Jake, her smile creeping up in a devious fashion on one side of her face.

"You probably should stay," she said reaching over to lay one hand on Jake's shoulder, "but you don't have to sleep on the couch if you don't want to."

Jake chuckled and shook his head. "Am I being propositioned, or is that the wine talking?"

"Probably both," Maddy answered, "but the offer still stands."

Jake leaned in, put his right arm around her shoulder, and pulled her gently toward him. As their lips touched, Jake felt as if he were melting. In the back of his mind Jake knew he'd wanted to do that for a long time, but feelings of friendship and respect for Maddy and her late husband had prevented him.

When their lips finally parted, Jake tilted his head back just a bit, looking into Maddy's deep green eyes. A little smile curled up the corners of his mouth as he shook his head. "Maddy," Jake said, "we've just polished off two bottles of wine. And while I care for you more than any woman I've ever known, I don't want to be the guy who took advantage of the slightly tipsy widow of one of the most up-standing citizens of Butterfield. Let's sleep on it…in separate rooms. Just toss me a blanket and I'll be sawing logs here on the couch in no time."

"Jake, Jake, Jake" Maddy's slightly slurry speech made the '*Js*' sound a little more like '*Sh's*'. "Sometimes I wish you weren't such a darn gentleman. It must be tough being so perfect."

"Perfectly drunk," Jake replied, "and perfectly exhausted."

Maddy got up and walked to a hall closet where she grabbed a blanket…walked back…and tossed it over Jake's head. "Here you go killjoy."

"Believe me Maddy," Jake said in a muffled voice with the blanket still on his head…"You'll thank me in the morning."

"Yeah, yeah, yeah," Maddy muttered as her voice trailed off

down the hallway. From that night on Jake and Maddy became a whole lot more than just friends.

* * *

But right now it was Maddy's friendship and her expertise as an attorney that Jake needed more than her passion. Maddy would be able to help Jake sift through all of the evidence he had amassed over the past few days.

"Okay," said Maddy, "now that your Jeep is safely hidden away in my garage…want to tell me what all this secrecy is about?"

"You look so good, I almost hate to get down to business right away," said Jake.

"Business before pleasure…would you like something to drink?"

"A cold beer would really hit the spot right now."

They walked down a short hallway that led to the kitchen, Maddy's bare feet making small soft slapping sounds on the tile floor.

In the kitchen, Maddy turned to give Jake a half smile and a little shake of the head. "You're serious about all this aren't you?"

Maddy opened the door on a large almond colored refrigerator and grabbed a bottle of beer. She twisted the top and handed it to Jake.

"Unfortunately, Maddy, I'm dead serious."

She reached back in the refrigerator and found a large bottle of white wine. Next to the bottle of wine was a small row of goblets. She picked up one of the chilled glasses, poured herself a glass of wine and put the bottle back in the fridge.

With Maddy leading the way, the two walked from the kitchen through the breakfast nook and into the den. Maddy had a fire burning. Jake collapsed into the large sofa. He took a long pull from the bottle of beer as Maddy sat down on the other end of the couch. She tucked one leg underneath her, took a sip of wine, and waited for Jake to begin.

"It all started a few days ago," Jake began, "with a phone call from the widow of a shooting victim whose body was found outside of town...in an empty field."

Jake laid out the whole story, from the death of Maria Sandoval to the late night discovery of what he believed to be a drug deal going down. When Jake told her who the license plate belonged to, Maddy didn't even flinch. She continued to absorb the details as Jake laid them out, like the consummate attorney that she was. It wasn't until Jake told her about the death of Billy Denton that Maddy broke her silence.

"So you think Billy's death was no accident, and that Detective Doogan had something to do with it?"

"I'm sure of it Maddy. You should have heard him on the phone. He as much as said the same thing could happen to me if I didn't watch my step. And he's not the only one telling me I should keep my nose out of this thing."

Jake told Maddy about the mysterious man in the dark suit who had confronted him in Rick Rollins' bar. A man who drove away in a large white Chevy sedan...a man who seemed to know every move that Jake had made over the past couple of days. Jake continued with what he'd learned during his golf game with Mick Williams about the Highway Patrol drug busts that were never prosecuted by the District Attorney's Office.

"So there it is, Maddy. You're my attorney, what do you make of it?"

Maddy got up and took Jake's empty beer bottle and her empty wine glass into the kitchen for a couple of refills. She returned with a fresh glass of white wine in one hand and a cold bottle of beer in the other. She handed Jake the beer and sat down on the edge of the oak coffee table facing Jake.

"Sounds like you've gotten yourself into quite a mess, and somebody's watching. I guess it *was* a good idea for you to park in my garage."

Maddy set her glass of wine on the coffee table and went over to the fireplace. She picked up a small log from a stack on the raised brick hearth and tossed it on top of the burning embers. She stabbed at the fire a couple of times with a poker and came back to the coffee table and sat down again.

"Okay," Maddy began, "you've got the District Attorney letting three drug busts go un-prosecuted. You've got a Detective in the Sheriff's Department not following up on five murders he must know are connected. And you've got the same detective possibly committing murder himself. Then you've got what looks like a drug deal going down, and the mayor's car is involved. And to top it all off, some mysterious dark suited guy with slicked-back hair is cornering you in a bar telling you to keep your nose out of it. Jake this is fantastic stuff."

"Maddy," Jake said, "the first thing that popped into my head when I saw that license plate this afternoon was the three amigos. Do you know what I'm talking about?"

"I know exactly what you're talking about. And that might be a great place to start putting this puzzle together. And I might be able to offer some insight into one of those amigos myself."

CHAPTER 22

It was 1966. The Butterfield High School football team was the best it had been in decades. Everybody in town was following the undefeated season, and everyone knew that a state championship was well within the team's grasp. The final game of the season would be between the Butterfield Eagles and the Fresno Wildcats, a high school with a rough reputation and an undefeated season of their own to brag about.

The main reason that Butterfield High had such a good team was the talent of three of its seniors. These three gifted athletes were affectionately referred to as the three amigos. They were not only responsible for most of the Eagle's scoring, they were also best friends, on and off the field.

Hord Matthews was the son of a prominent local attorney. He lived a fairly pampered youth. He drove a new car to school as soon as he got his drivers license. He was a straight "A" student but with a wild streak that got the three young men in trouble on more than one occasion, but not so much trouble that his father couldn't get him, and his friends, off the hook. Hord was the Eagle's quarterback. He would eventually follow in his father's footsteps, going off to college to get a law degree.

Clay Sanderson played wide receiver on the team. He was tall and fast, and at six-foot-four, he was the main target of Hord Matthew's passing game. Hord knew that if you got the ball somewhere in the vicinity of the pass catcher's long arms, big hands, and towering stature, the lanky Sanderson would be the one who came down with the ball, and oftentimes that was in the end zone. Clay Sanderson's father was a Deputy Sheriff. He was close to retirement when Clay became a senior, and it was common knowledge that Clay would follow in his father's footsteps and get into law enforcement when high school was over. When it came to getting the exuberant threesome out of a fix every now and then, having a parent that wore a badge didn't hurt either.

The third member of the three amigos was Sam Poole. Sam came from a broken home. His mother worked as a secretary. Sam's father had walked out on the family when Sam was just three years old. He'd never seen his father, and had no recollection of him ever being around. His mother had destroyed all pictures of Sam's father, and she never spoke of him or their ill-fated marriage. Sam Poole was the running back on the football team. His shiftiness both on and off the field earned him the nickname "Sam the Sham" after a rock group named "Sam the Sham and the Pharaohs" that had a 1965 hit titled "Wooly Bully." It was said that Sam Poole could con his own grandmother out of her dentures. It was a trait that would serve Sam well later in life. Sam set the Butterfield High School record his senior year for yardage gained on the ground. He was short and stocky...swift and shifty...and hard to stop, either at the line of scrimmage or in the open field.

As the state championship showdown between Butterfield and Fresno approached, the entire town was decorated with green and gold. Every image of an eagle that the townsfolk could lay their hands on was adorning everything from automobiles to office buildings. There was even a billboard near downtown with a huge Eagle...talons bared...that read "Good Luck Eagles." Fresno was the odds on favorite to win, especially since Butterfield had to travel to the Wildcat's stadium to play the final game. They outweighed Butterfield by about fifteen pounds per man, and all the local papers didn't give the Eagles much of a chance. But on that cold and hazy Saturday night in Fresno, with thousands of people yelling wildly, the game was never even close. The three amigos took the game over from their first possession. When the final gun sounded, the Eagles were the new state champs, by a convincing score of 45 to 21. They were the heroes of the entire city of Butterfield.

High School graduation though would take the three best friends their separate ways, but Butterfield hadn't heard the last of the three amigos.

Hord Matthews kept the family tradition by attending law school at Harvard.

Clay Sanderson attended a local junior college before finishing up his law enforcement degree at San Francisco State. Sam Poole stayed in Butterfield. He tried the junior college route for a short time, but football was the only thing that enticed him into a classroom, and after a knee injury, his football career and his education came to a grinding halt. The only good thing that came from the knee surgery for Sam was that it kept him out of the draft and out of Vietnam. Without football and school to occupy his time, Sam went in search of employment.

Sam was still close enough to the glory days of that State Championship that a number of job offers came his way. He settled on working for a local Ford dealership. It didn't take long for Sam the Sham to find out he was good at selling cars to people. New cars, used cars, it didn't matter, Sam could sell a set of wheels to anyone who walked onto the lot. And it didn't take Sam long to figure out that there was more money to be made by selling his own cars. Within a couple of years, Sam's Used Cars opened for business just down the street from the Ford dealership.

Soon, there was a second used car lot with Sam's name on it, and then came Sam's Furniture and Appliance followed by Sam's Audio/Video City. By the time Hord Matthews and Clay Sanderson returned to make their mark on Butterfield just about everyone in town owned something they'd purchased from Sam Poole. Sam would have been a multi-millionaire in no time except for two major character flaws. He loved the women and he loved gambling. After three divorces and far too many trips to Las Vegas, Sam Poole was doling out as much money as he was taking in. But as everyone in Butterfield would say, "well, that's Sam Poole for you. He's still a helluva' guy."

Hord Matthews returned from Harvard Law School, passed the California Bar Exam, and joined his father's law practice. The firm was very successful. "Matthews and Matthews" had some of the biggest names in town as clients, but after a number of years in the business, Hord Matthews was ready for a new challenge. He ran for San Jacinto County District Attorney, and won in a landslide.

While Hord Matthews was carving out a successful law career, Clay Sanderson was working his way up the law enforcement ladder. He became best known for his revamping of, and becoming spokesman for, the San Jacinto County Search and Rescue Team which helped locate the adventurous novices who often got lost in the adjacent mountains. His next successful task was spearheading the County's Drug

Enforcement Division. Drugs had slowly become a nasty big city thorn in the community's side, and Clay Sanderson was determined to nip it in the bud. Every time there was a bust, the drugs, guns, and cash, were proudly displayed to the local media. With all the notoriety Clay obtained, and with a natural born sense of how to say the right thing in front of a news camera, the next logical step for Clay was to run for San Jacinto County Sheriff, and with the backing of his former football teammate and current District Attorney, Clay Sanderson became the new Sheriff.

Two of the three amigos had now achieved a great deal success in the local political arena, but the third, Sam Poole, was still a struggling entrepreneur. His golden touch at business had gotten about as tarnished as his luck in love. But one of his community service ventures finally put him in a position to be the third part of the three amigos' triangle.

Sam had volunteered to be part of the new Butterfield Economic Development Association, whose job it was to go out of the county and lure new businesses into the area with tax incentives and promises of cheap land. Just like in the old days of selling cars, Sam Poole found that his gift of gab and knack for barter made him the perfect economic ambassador for the Butterfield area. Within a few years, Sam's economic expeditions netted the local business community everything from a new potato chip manufacturing plant to the headquarters for a major national insurance company. It wasn't long before Sam Poole was being named Man-of-the-Year. And Sam, seeing a pot of gold at the end of his current rainbow, parlayed his new-found celebrity status into a run for the Mayor's office. And with the solid backing of the Sheriff and the District Attorney, not only did Sam Poole become the next Mayor of Butterfield, he ran for the office unopposed.

So, there they were. The same threesome that brought the state football championship to Butterfield were back together again, taking the City of Butterfield into the future.

CHAPTER 23

"The three amigos" Maddy said. She wasn't seated on the edge of the coffee table any longer. Maddy prowled the carpet in the den as if she were in a courtroom making her case to the jury. "But why. They're high powered, well-respected citizens. And they don't need the money. At least two of them don't. So why would they be selling drugs and murdering drug dealers?"

"What do you mean 'at least two of them don't ?'" asked Jake.

"It's the one thing that rang a bell when you first brought up our three illustrious city leaders." Maddy walked back toward the kitchen to refill her wine glass. "Another beer Jake?"

"No thanks. What rang a bell?"

Maddy poured herself another glass of wine and walked slowly back into the den. She lifted the glass to her mouth for a small sip while she stared into the fireplace, watching the sparks from the crackling fire disappear up the chimney, lifted by the hot air. She turned to look at Jake, her face deep in thought.

"Mayor Poole," said Maddy, letting the name dangle in the air for a moment. She continued…"According to some of my acquaintances, our Mister Poole has been living far beyond his means."

"For instance," said Jake.

"Word has it that Sam Poole was just about bankrupt when he won the Mayor's race. He was still paying child support and alimony to two of his three wives, and he hadn't had a truly successful business venture in some time. And the job as Mayor may be prestigious, but it doesn't pay all that much. But Sam Poole moved into a luxurious home here on the west side just a few months ago. He's also driving a new Mercedes. And from what I gather he isn't being subsidized by the new love of his life."

"Sound like it fits the puzzle," said Jake.

"But still Jake," Maddy returned to the sofa, once again folding her right leg underneath her. She set her wine glass on the coffee table. "I have to look at the hard facts of this thing. It's what I do for a living. You strongly suspect Detective Doogan because of his tone of voice on the phone. And we know the suited man with the slicked back hair in the bar was no hallucination. But the rest is still circumstantial. There could be no investigation into your five murders for a number of valid reasons. The same could be true for the CHP drug busts that never got prosecuted. And the Mayor's car, maybe somebody has access to it other than Poole."

"That's a lot of circumstantial if you ask me, Maddy."

"Yeah…but if your suspicions are correct, where do we go from here? I mean, we'd have to take this to the Attorney General. You're one big problem is that most of the local authorities are also suspects." Maddy reached for the glass of wine. "Do we have anything else?"

Jake thought for a moment…"Only what Billy told me he found in the files of the five murder victims."

"What was that?" asked Maddy.

"There were three .22 caliber shell casings at each of the murder scenes. And they all had three sets of cowboy boot prints."

"Hmmm," Maddy thought, "interesting. .22 caliber is not the usual weapon of choice for law enforcement. I don't think that would be what your Detective Doogan would be carrying around in his shoulder holster. Maybe that's what slick in the dark suit carries. But the cowboy boots, that's really odd. Detectives usually wear those plain leather lace-up street shoes, most of them not very noticeable. What did your friend in the bar have on?"

"I don't know," Jake answered. "But I'm pretty sure they weren't cowboy boots."

"Cowboy boots to me," Maddy said, "sounds like whoever killed the five drug dealers may have hired some good 'ol boys to do the job. I wish there was some way we could get our three amigos together to see what their reaction would be with you in the room."

Jake shook his head and laughed.

"What's so funny?" asked Maddy.

"Ask and ye shall receive," said Jake. "I'm emceeing a fundraiser tomorrow night at the Civic Center for the Rescue Mission. According to the program I was sent, all three are supposed to be there."

CHAPTER 24

Jake pulled into the Convention Center parking lot around six thirty. The fundraiser started at seven. In front of the Center stood a large brightly lit electronic sign. Mustard Yellow computer generated letters crawled across the black background of the sprawling billboard which read…"Rescue Mission Gala Dinner." This was not a night Jake was looking forward to. Not only was he likely to confront three men who might be key figures in something that had turned his life upside down, but he also had to wear a tuxedo. Jake hated tuxedoes. He considered the "penguin suit" a uniform that was a necessary evil to fulfill his duties as emcee. Climbing out of his Jeep, Jake grabbed the double breasted tux jacket from the passengers seat, adjusted his black vest, and headed toward the large double glass doors of the Civic Center.

Down a long thickly carpeted hallway, Jake entered the double-doors of a large ballroom where scores of Civic Center employees in dark slacks, white shirts and black bow ties, scurried around carrying everything from silverware to pitchers of water. Over a hundred tables were set up, each decorated with colorful helium filled balloons attached to flowery centerpieces. Neatly folded linen napkins, mock crystal goblets, and perfectly placed dinnerware surrounded bone white plates. The white linen tablecloths were covered with multi-colored confetti and ornately printed programs of the evening's activities. At the front of the ballroom, technicians in gray uniforms arranged chairs and tested the microphone that sat atop an oak podium at the center of the large stage. Behind the stage was a large white screen on which pictures and video of the Rescue Mission's many accomplishments would be shown to the hundreds of guests who would be thanked for their many contributions, and asked to contribute even more.

At the back of the auditorium stood Father Donald Durbin. Dressed in a black suit and black shirt with a white clerics collar, Father Durbin was the perfect figure of a man you would trust with your most personal of confessions. Padre Don, as his friends fondly referred to him, wasn't a tall man. He was stout, with a full head of wavy pure white hair with a matching moustache and beard, which was kept neatly trimmed, leaving his neck clean-shaven. He could show up on your rooftop on any Christmas Eve and nobody would ask for identification. Father Durbin was in serious conversation with a man in a dark gray Civic Center uniform who held a walkie-talkie in one hand as he gestured resolutely with the other. Most likely it was about some last minute detail that Father Durbin wanted taken care of before the hundreds of Rescue Mission paying faithful filtered in to partake of the three course meal, wine, and no-host cocktails. This was Father Durbin's shining moment in front of his Butterfield benefactors who helped fund his outreach program on the east side of town. Jake would love to tell Father Durbin how grateful he was that the Rescue Mission proved to be such great cover for his early morning foray into a drug deal that involved the mayor's car. Maybe Jake would be able to tell him on the news some night. A five piece jazz band on one side of the ballroom began playing softly as Jake walked toward Father Durbin. A broad smile overtook the Father's face as Jake approached. With an outstretched arm, Father Durbin grasped Jake's hand as the two came face to face.

"Jake," the handshake was firm and sincere. "So glad to see you. I can't tell you how grateful I am that you'll be hosting our event again tonight."

"It's always my pleasure," Jake said. "Looks like you're expecting a big crowd again."

"The good Lord provides," Father Durbin replied. He handed Jake two sheets of neatly printed paper. "Here's the rundown of the evening's events. Just the usual welcome and recognizing of some of the dignitaries who'll be in attendance tonight. You know the routine. Then turn it over to me."

Jake did know the routine. He'd emceed every fundraiser the Mission held since the first one six years ago. Jake looked at the sheets of paper. There were the names of local businesses and individuals that got special mention at the beginning of the evening. Then there were the names of dignitaries who would be in attendance, among them, the Mayor, the Sheriff, and the District Attorney.

It was approaching seven when the guests started arriving. "Guests" was hardly the appropriate word. After all, each person who walked into tonight's festivities, dressed in their best formal attire, had paid a hundred and fifty dollars for the mass menu of chicken and rice pilaf. They were the city's elite. And even though tonight's fund-raiser was one of the many ways the local rich got to hobnob with each other, the bottom line was that they were the financial backbone of much of the good that was done for the needy in Butterfield. And much to their credit, they always showed up for these events, and they always opened up their wallets to Padre Don.

As predictable as the rising of the tide, the celebrants began to file in, filling the quiet vacuum with a din of chatter. Four strategically placed bars were busy as bow-tied servers offered a variety of libations from gin and tonics to Corona's. Jake found his way to one of the alcohol outposts. A little fortification for the evening wasn't a bad idea. He ordered a Bud Light, and tried to give the bartender a five-dollar bill. "Drinks are on the house for you tonight Mister Adams," said a very polite young man.

"Thanks, no glass, the bottle will do fine," said Jake, as he dropped two dollars into a tip glass and headed back to the stage to go over his rundown.

As he walked toward the podium, Jake paused to talk with some of the evening's patrons who recognized the t-v anchorman. They were all glad to exchange a few words with their local celebrity. Jake always felt a little out of his league at these functions. "If I had their money..." Jake thought to himself, "I'd throw mine away."

Jake located a dinner table immediately in front of the stage with a small sign affixed to a brass holder that said "reserved." Jake found the small blue cardboard marker folded in half like a little tent that read "Jake Adams", and he sat down. Jake would be sitting at the front table with Father Durbin, not only to recognize Jake as the emcee of the evening, but also to give him easy access to the stage.

It was now a few minutes after seven, time for Jake to go to the microphone, welcome everyone, thank them for their kind attendance, and encourage them to have a great time. He would also use the vantage point of the stage as a crow's nest to see if he could locate any of the three players in his investigative soap opera. Jake wasn't sure if they would be seated in some prestigious location in the large ballroom, if they would be seated together, or if they would even show up for the fundraiser.

Jake took the two sheets of paper Father Durbin had given him and walked toward the steps on the side of the stage. Traversing the twenty feet or so to the podium, Jake let his eyes casually wander over the crowd. The hall was beginning to fill rapidly. Jake saw a lot of familiar faces in the growing numbers of tuxedos and evening dresses, but the three amigos were not among them. Arriving at the oak podium, Jake turned the microphone switch to the on position.

"Good evening everyone. My name is Jake Adams, your friendly neighborhood anchorman." A warm round of applause for the silver haired personality reverberated through the hall. "I just want to welcome all of you to this wonderful event benefiting one of the most worthwhile causes in the city. And I know that I can speak for Father Durbin when I say, 'please leave all of your money here tonight, don't take any of it home with you.'" The crowd broke out in laughter. "Have a great evening and a great dinner." Jake walked back off the stage and to his seat at the front table.

"Jake, it's great to have you here as our host tonight." A gray-haired gentleman caught Jake's attention just as he was about to sit down. It was Dr. Leo Bernard, a man Jake had met in the days when Ben Scofield was alive. "We sure do miss Ben, don't we?"

"There'll never be another like him," Jake replied. He reached to take another swallow of his beer and found it empty.

"As your physician I believe I have a remedy for that." Dr. Bernard took notice of Jake's barren beer bottle. "Why not let me buy you another?"

"Sounds like a great idea," said Jake. He and Dr. Bernard made their way to the nearest watering station. Jake ordered another Bud Light. Dr. Bernard ordered a double Jack Daniels on the rocks, and the two began an earnest discussion about the old days when Ben Scofield was alive.

Within half an hour the ballroom was packed with people. Dinner would be served at 7:30 and it was part of Jake's duties as emcee to announce that fact over the microphone. Jake arrived at the podium at the same time an army of bow-tied help began bringing trays full of salads to the tables.

"Sirs and Madams...dinner is served." Jakes eyes made another pass over the sea of faces in formal attire, and bingo! Over to the far right, about half way down the long row of tables, Jake's radar picked up its first recognizable blip. The balding man with a stocky build stood in the middle of a small group of people, making some sort of resolute point using both hands and a large unlit cigar for emphasis. Mayor Sam Poole was holding court. No sooner had Jake zeroed in on one his targets for the evening, than the other two came into view. Just behind the Mayor, at the next table, stood the Sheriff, Clay Sanderson and District Attorney Hord Matthews. They were alone, in conversation with one another.

The rather bizarre urge to just walk right up and interrogate them popped into Jake's mind. He, of course, didn't entertain that notion for long. Instead he decided to join the others at his table for dinner. Jake made his way off the platform, passing Father Durbin who was on his way up to the microphone to deliver the pre-meal prayer, one that would thank God both for the blessings already received and the ones yet to come.

The roasted chicken with a honey sauce was delicious. The desert was chocolate mousse. Desert was Jake's cue to head back to the podium and begin the program. After all the honored guests were recognized, including the three amigos,

Jake gave his own modest observations of how important the Rescue Mission was to the community, and how honored he was to be a part of their fundraiser each year. He then turned the program over to Father Durbin.

The agenda included a slide show of the improvements at the Mission; videotaped testimony from people who had gotten off the streets and back into the mainstream of life with the Mission's help; ending with a former drug addict and single mother of three who had finally turned her life around because of Father Durbin's help. The very personal and emotional story of drugs, an abusive father, and losing and regaining custody of her children brought most of the audience to tears. It was just the mood Father Durbin wanted as he returned to the rostrum to deliver a short but fiery sermon on the necessity of giving 'till it hurts in order to take away the pain of the less fortunate. The Father's words were greeted with explosive applause followed by the furious search for checkbooks and pens.

Jake returned to the microphone to thank everyone for attending the evening's events and to remind everyone to place their kind contributions in the small wicker basket at the center of each table. He also reminded them that they were more than welcome to stay and dance the night away to the sound of the small jazz band. He said a short goodnight and walked off the stage.

At the back of the auditorium was a large collage of pictures pasted on white poster board perched on three separate easels depicting the work of the Rescue Mission. Father Durbin had made his way to that display. Well-wishers came by to give their thanks and words of encouragement, and to take an occasional picture with the gray-haired padre. As he neared the back of the hall, Jake stopped about ten feet short of where the Padre was standing. Next to Father Durbin, smiling broadly for the photographer were the three main characters in Jake's investigative saga. Jake stood his ground as the three amigos and Father Durbin posed for pictures and exchanged pleasantries. As Jake debated whether to say goodnight or just turn and go, something caught his eye. He wasn't exactly sure what it was that made him look down. Some voice from inside; some gut feeling that forced his eyes to move from the smiling, talking faces to the floor. Jake's heart and breath felt like they were suddenly put on hold. There they were. The Mayor, the District Attorney, and the Sheriff...and they were all wearing cowboy boots.

The blood seemed to rush out of Jake's face. He felt a chill; no, a numbness, engulf his entire body. Madeline Scofield would say it was just more piece of circumstantial evidence. Jake knew better, and he knew it in his heart. These three men, standing before him in all their bureaucratic splendor, were murderers...and drug dealers...and God knows what else. They were the ones who had left what little evidence there was at the crime scenes.

Jakes eyes were now riveted to the cowboy boots. Realizing that he was transfixed by what these three men were wearing, Jake's eyes rose. His gaze was met directly by Hord Matthews, the District Attorney. The prosecutor's eyes, underneath thick black eyebrows, were staring straight back at Jake. A small smile crept up one side of the DA-s mouth.

"Jake Adams," Matthews said, "you look like you've seen a ghost. Are you alright?"

Jake collected his thoughts quickly, a skill he'd developed over the years when things fell apart during a live broadcast.

"I'm fine Mister District Attorney. It's just so...well, so...good to see all of you together for such a great cause." Jake reverted to his old trick of injecting a little sarcasm into what was an obviously tense situation. Perusing all three faces, which now focused directly in on him, Jake continued on his present course.

"I know how busy you all are...and I know Father Durbin is especially happy that you could take time out of your busy schedules to be here."

Father Durbin gave a polite smile, completely unaware of the depth of the conversation.

"But I'm sure," Hord Matthews deadpanned, never releasing his eye contact with Jake, "that you've been just as busy lately. Am I right Jake?"

Despite the tone of the conversation, Jake couldn't help but feel a grin forming as he faced the most powerful political figures he could imagine in a small town like Butterfield. "Yes, I have. It's just the nature of the business of being an investigative reporter I'm afraid."

"I'm sure it is," replied Matthews.

The District Attorney was the most formidable looking of the three men. The former high school quarterback was still in good shape. A slight hint of gray peppered the sides of his black hair. He had dark intense eyes, and a dead serious look that served him well as the county's leading prosecutor. Next to Hord Matthews stood the San Jacinto County Sheriff, Clay Sanderson. Matthews and Sanderson were often on the nightly news together. Drug busts and homicide investigations often brought them in front of the cameras to update the public on their latest achievement. Sanderson was the taller of the three at about six foot four. The slender Sheriff, even at sixty years old still had a youthful look about him. A shock of red hair and a ruddy complexion with a hint of freckles helped to disguise his age. Small flecks of gray in his red moustache were the only things that would make you think Sanderson was much older than forty-five. Rounding out the threesome (and rounding was the right word) was the Mayor, Sam Poole. Poole stood about five foot ten and weighed about two hundred-fifty pounds. His girth and rosy complexion reflected his disdain for physical activity a love of good food and adult beverages. The Mayor was completely bald. Even without the daily use of a razor, Sam Poole would have precious little hair adorning the sides and back of his head. It was his ardent opinion that he looked much more mayoral with a completely hairless pate, not unlike being the Daddy Warbucks of the City of Butterfield.

Jake maintained his position as he turned his attention to Father Durbin. "I just wanted to thank you for another great evening before I go Father."

"Why no, Jake," Father Durbin walked over to grasp Jake's hand, "thank you. This event just wouldn't be the same without your generous contribution as emcee. Are you sure you won't stay and have a drink with us?"

"No thanks, I'd better get going."

The two shook hands. Jake turned to the three local leaders who just stood there, looking like they were posing for a Who's Who portrait.

"Gentlemen," Jake offered a crisp nod of the head and turned to leave.

Jake's heart pounded as he walked down the carpeted hallway. Reaching the double glass doors, Jake pushed on one of the long chrome handles, and as the cold evening air hit his face, he just stood there for a moment, letting the chill of the night refresh his senses which had been on auto pilot for the past few moments. Pausing to collect his thoughts, Jake quickly noticed that the fog had once again settled in…gobbling up everything in the valley. The fog-muffled sound of a train whistle moaned somewhere in the distance. It gave an eerily audible punctuation mark to the night. Jake made his way to his Jeep…unlocked the door and climbed in. He fired up the Wrangler and pushed the heater knob to its farthest position. A light layer of drizzle had formed on the Jeep, and Jake had to turn on the windshield wipers before heading out of the parking lot.

Jake made the short drive from downtown to his house to pick up a few things. He would have dumped the tuxedo, but he didn't want to waste the time changing. He grabbed a beer from the fridge and called Maddy, who was reluctantly impressed with Jake's cowboy boot observation. She was, as Jake would have predicted, not as eager to jump to conclusions. Jake still felt that staying out of sight would be his best option. He told Maddy that he was going to put a few things in a sports bag and be right over. Jake took long pulls from the bottle of Bud Light as he tossed clothes into the black nylon bag with the Nike logo on it. He zipped up the bag and hoisted the strap up over his shoulder. He chugged the last of his beer, tossed the empty bottle in a plastic trashcan in the kitchen and headed back out the front door.

As the front door locked behind him, Jake stood for a moment, listening to the soundless night. Even with Jake's sarcastic bravado of a short time ago, he did fear for his safety enough to exercise some caution. He didn't know what he was listening for, maybe the sound of an idling car engine or the muffled sound of footsteps. There was nothing. He tossed the bag of clothes into the passenger seat of the Jeep and headed to Maddy's. In just a few seconds Jake would be out of his neighborhood and headed toward the safe haven of Maddy's home.

There was only the faint glow of a few sets of headlights as Jake approached Riverside Drive, the road that would take him out to the southwest part of town with the minimal amount of stoplights. Jake made the turn onto Riverside and suddenly the surrounding fog seemed to light up like a pinball machine, and in his mirror Jake saw the source of the kaleidoscope of color. He was being pulled over. The first thing that jumped into Jake's mind was wondering who was in the car. It even crossed his mind to make a run for it. But he decided against the idea. Instead, he pulled over to the side of the road.

Blinded by the revolving red, yellow, and blue lights, Jake heard a car door slam, and in his sideview mirror he saw a uniformed silhouette approaching his Jeep. He rolled down the window and waited.

CHAPTER 25

With his immediate surroundings lit up like a Christmas tree, Jake didn't get a good look at just who'd pulled him over until the officer reached his open window. It was the brown uniform of a Sheriff's Deputy. Jake spoke first.

"Good evening officer, is there something wrong?"

"Could I see your driver's license and registration, please?" The deputy was firm yet polite.

"Certainly." Jake opened his glove box, grabbed an envelope with a cellophane window that contained his registration. He handed that to the deputy while he reached inside the console between the Jeep's bucket seats to find his wallet. He plucked the driver's license out of the billfold and handed it to the officer. The deputy smelled of cologne or after-shave. Jake assumed the patrolman had just come on duty. All Jake could see at present was a shiny brass badge attached to a very well starched uniform.

"Do you know why I stopped you Mister Adams?" asked the officer.

"No," replied Jake, trying to be as cordial as possible, "I don't, to be honest with you."

"Have you ever heard of a California stop Mister Adams? I'm afraid that's why I pulled you over. You not only didn't come to a complete stop back there, you just rolled right through the stop sign like it wasn't there."

"I'm awfully sorry, officer," Jake tried to put on his best defense. "I just came from a big fundraiser at the Civic Center, and I guess trying to thread my way through this fog made me a little inattentive."

"Well, Mister Adams, rolling through stop signs in this kind of fog can be very dangerous." There was a short pause, and then the rather young sounding deputy took a very serious tone. "Mister Adams...have you been drinking?"

Jake knew better than to lie, and he knew that a quick response was his best response. "I had a couple of beers at tonight's fundraiser for the Rescue Mission at the Civic Center." Jake thought a little subtle psychology might work. "In fact, you're boss was there...Clay Sanderson. I emceed the event. My license says Jacob Allen Adams, but I go by Jake. Jake Adams, the local television anchorman."

"I see." The deputy seemed to mull over the situation for a moment...then, "Well, I'm afraid, Mister Adams, that I don't' watch much T-V...and I'm fairly new to the area. Could you step out of the car please?"

"Certainly," replied Jake. Out of the Jeep he was now face to face with a young man no more than twenty-five with short blond hair and moustache and small brown eyes. Those eyes were looking directly into Jake's.

The officer reached for something from his utility belt and spoke to Jake in his matter-of-fact monotone. "Just keep your eyes open for a moment Mister Adams."

Suddenly Jake's eyes were staring straight into the intense beam of a small flashlight. Jake quickly realized his eyes would at least reflect the fact that his recent nights had been anything but restful. That combined with the alcohol on his breath made Jake a bit concerned about his current situation. The young deputy wasn't about to alter that state of mind.

"Mister Adams, you're eyes are very bloodshot, and I'm afraid that under the circumstances, with alcohol on your breath, and the fact that you ran a stop sign in these extremely foggy conditions, I really have no alternative but to take you downtown."

Jake figured it was time to pull out all the stops if he was to get out of this predicament. "I'm not arguing," he said, "but I don't have as much as an outstanding parking ticket in this town. Maybe you could call in and check. I'm sure someone there can vouch for my credibility."

"I'm sure they can, Mister Adams. And maybe when we get downtown, they'll just write this off as an unfortunate experience and send you home. But I have to do my job." The next words were not what Jake wanted to hear. "Would you please turn around and put your hands behind your back. I'm going to have to handcuff you and let the folks downtown make any further decisions."

With no practical options, Jake did as the officer requested. The young deputy pulled a set of stainless steel handcuffs from a leather holder on his belt, placed them securely on Jake's wrists and led him to the rear door of the patrol car.

Once inside, the deputy took the handset from his two-way radio. "This is Patrol 631. I have a possible DUI in custody. Name, Jacob Allen Adams, drivers license SO328459."

There was no response on the other end. The deputy put the patrol car in gear. They drove along a series of traffic islands and at the next available left turn lane, the young deputy made a sharp U-turn back toward downtown. Jake kept watch through the rear windows, but as they approached the downtown area where the County Jail was located, the deputy suddenly took another left.

For the first time, Jake felt a knot form in his stomach. The deputy wasn't heading for the County Jail. "I've lived here long enough to know that this isn't the way to the County Jail." Jake felt like he was talking to a cab driver who might be taking the wrong route in order to get a bigger fare.

"I'm sorry Mister Adams," replied the still stoic deputy, "but I have one more stop to make before we head to booking."

Booking…what a lovely word, Jake thought. Still he wasn't completely comfortable with the way things were panning out right now. Where was this destination? He was, after all, in the clutches of a deputy that worked for someone who might like Jake out of the way…for good.

The young deputy drove only a few short blocks before he took a sharp right into a two level parking garage adjacent to the Bank of America. At eleven-thirty at night it would be empty. So, what appointment did this rookie officer have in the middle of the night in a vacant parking structure in Downtown Butterfield? Jake felt that any questions now would be a waste of his vocal chords, so he just watched as the concrete scenery took him and his uniformed chauffeur up to the top level of the parking garage.

At the top of the ramp, there was no more concrete ceiling, only open air, filled with the dead calm of the late night fog. Jake's mindset had now changed. He sensed that something was wrong, but he kept his wits about him.

His senses were right. As the deputy's patrol car finished its trek up the ramp leading to the second parking tier, the pavement leveled off and Jake saw the yellow parking lights of two vehicles.

The deputy remained silent as he pulled the patrol car to a stop in front of the two large white Chevy sedans. The young officer quietly exited the auto and walked to the rear door and opened it. "Would you please step out, Mister Adams?"

"Why would I want to get out here?" asked Jake.

"I'm afraid it's not your decision. Please get out."

Jake got out of the back seat. As he stood up, his hands still wearing the cold stainless steel bracelets, Jake heard an all too familiar voice. "Jake, Jake, Jake…what in the world are we going to do with you?" He'd heard that voice on numerous occasions on the evening news…and just a short time ago at the Rescue Mission fundraiser. It was the voice of the District Attorney, Hord Matthews.

From behind the two sedans, four men came into view. The Mayor, the Sheriff, and the D-A Jake knew immediately. The fourth looked familiar, but he couldn't put a name to the face. Then it came to him.

"This is a heck of way to get together," Jake said, "after such a lovely evening. This is Detective Doogan, I presume."

Doogan's gravelly voice sounded like it was growling. "Nice to see you Jake".

"Frisk him, then take the cuffs off him," said the District Attorney. "I don't think we have too much to worry about."

The young deputy patted Jake down then grabbed a set of keys from his utility belt and unlocked the handcuffs. Jake rubbed each of his wrists. "Cowboy boots." Jake said.

"What's that about cowboy boots, Jake?" asked the D-A.

"The three sets of prints at the crime scenes…they were made by cowboy boots. That's what kind of put it together for me tonight." Jake shook his head. "You guys got a lotta' balls.

I'm not sure the people who elected you to office would approve however."

The mayor, Sam Poole, let out a somewhat surprising belly laugh. "Jake my boy, I must say I admire your sense of humor at a time like this."

"Oh yeah," Jake responded, "I'm just a laugh riot. One question though, if you don't mind. Why? I mean, killing drug dealers, taking over the local drug trade...what in the world's gotten into you guys?"

"Well, Jake," the D-A spoke up again. "I guess since you've come this far I could give you a quick answer. Too bad it will never make the evening news however."

"Oh," Jake shot back," never underestimate the power of the press."

Hord Matthews chuckled. "You see Jake, the question is not why we did it, the question is why not. Let me explain. I've been the District Attorney here for quite some time now. And a big part of that has been prosecuting these scumbag drug dealers. But you see, they're like cockroaches, Jake. As soon as you put two or three in jail, another bunch of 'em come crawling out of the woodwork."

"Ask Clay here. He's probably arrested the same perps over and over again. Sometimes, Jake, this justice system of ours is nothing more than a revolving door. And that means that me and Clay are just spinning our wheels. But the real question is why? Why do these drug dealers keep showing up? Sure it's the money. But the money wouldn't be there if these idiot citizens here in Butterfield didn't want this stuff. Don't you see, Jake? It's really just the age-old principle of supply and demand. So no matter how much work we do in trying to get the drugs and the dealers off the streets, we'll never be able to do it."

"So then one day, the three of us were on a little fishing trip, and I just asked one very simple question to Clay and Sam here.

I said, 'if the illustrious citizens of Butterfield are going to keep on buying this stuff, why shouldn't we be the ones selling it to them?'"

The D-A continued, getting more and more wrapped up in his dissertation on drug dealing in Butterfield. "It was like a light went on, Jake. I mean, we had all the connections. We knew most of the drug dealers on a first name basis. All we had to do was get some of the local suppliers out of the way and it's clear sailin'. If the money's going to be made, why shouldn't we make it."

"We've busted our butts for years and the stuff still keeps coming in. So we'll be the ones to give them whatever it is they're hooked on, and we'll put the cash in our pocket. After all, Jake, we are the law around here. I don't see anybody standing in our way." The D-A quieted himself for a moment and looked straight at Jake. "Well, maybe one standing in our way. But that will be short lived."

"But why the Sandoval woman…and why my friend Billy?" Jake asked.

"Simple, Jake." Matthew's mood had become much more sinister. "They put our operation as risk…just like you do."

Jake was thankful for the D-A's somewhat lengthy speech, not because he was truly interested in the D-A's rather twisted sense of logic. Jake had used the time to make an assessment of his current situation. He had no intention of getting in anybody's patrol car again. They probably had another field already picked out somewhere outside of town, where Jake would be found still wearing the tuxedo he never took the time to remove. But Jake had other plans. They could shoot him in the back if they wanted, but some sort of escape on foot seemed like the next logical step. There was one big problem however. Behind Jake stood the young deputy and in front of him stood four men who had no intention of letting Jake slip through their hands.

But Jake had done something quite by instinct on his way up to the top level of the parking garage that he hoped would serve him well now. During his years of four-wheeling into the wilderness Jake developed the habit of being very aware of his surroundings. Getting lost on some old back road could turn a pleasurable expedition into a nightmare. So Jake always paid close attention to his surroundings on the way in, so he wouldn't get lost on the way out.

As Hord Matthews was delivering his diatribe on drugs and death, Jake was going over the layout of the parking garage in his mind. On the other side of the young deputy's patrol car was the ramp that led back down to the lower level of the garage. To keep people from driving off into the abyss created by the descending ramp there was a short concrete wall a few feet high. With this knowledge in hand, Jake's plan was simple, and it was about to go into action. With the D-A's last comment, all eyes were presently on Jake. Quickly trying to shift the focus, Jake zeroed in on the rotund Mayor.

"But Sam Poole, why you? How did you get mixed up in all this? How did you let these two high ranking thugs suck you into this mess?" The question was terse and delivered with Jake's best venomous voice. It was meant to bite, to put the Mayor on the spot, figuring Poole was the weak link in the operation. Jake was right. All eyes quickly turned to see what the Mayor's response would be. Sam Poole in fact, was caught off guard by the question. His face flushed in response. Sam Poole was now the focus of everyone's attention. Poole himself then looked over into the faces of his two cronies, searching for an answer to Jake's question. It was at that split second, with all eyes diverted, that Jake leaped into action. In one swift motion,

Jake turned and planted both of his hands firmly on the hood of the patrol car and vaulted over the top. Before the others knew what was happening, Jake's butt landed on the far front fender. He pushed himself away from the patrol car with both hands and made a dash for the center of the small concrete wall. At that point of the wall, the exit ramp would be several feet below him according to Jake's hasty calculations.

Jake heard the voices yelling behind him as he made his escape, but like a pro football player trying to get the ball into the end zone, Jake paid no attention to the chaotic cries behind him. His focus was on one small stretch of concrete, now just a few feet away. Jake reached the three-foot high guardrail, and with both hands on the top of the rough surface, he leaped over. He'd guessed well. After a fall of about four feet, the bottoms of his rented patent leather shoes hit the ramp below. The slick leather soles slipped on the concrete. Jake's butt hit the ground as he braced himself against the fall with the palms of his hands.

Jake figured that even if they gave chase on foot, the others wouldn't risk jumping over the concrete railing. Whoever followed him would likely approach the exit ramp from the top, and give chase from there. He was right. As Jake righted himself, he took a quick look back. Just entering the top of the ramp was Detective Doogan. Doogan had a sneer on his face and a nickel-plated revolver in his hand.

Jake sprinted to the concrete railing that separated the exit ramp from the ground level below. At the point Jake approached the wall, he realized that this jump would be more like eight or ten feet. But Jake was in luck. As he neared the railing, a large Chevy Tahoe was parked directly below. Once again planting his hands on the top of the concrete, Jake launched himself over and into the air. Just as his feet left the ground Jake heard the crack of gunfire. Doogan had squeezed off two rounds from his revolver. Jake heard the projectiles slam into the nearby concrete as his feet landed on the hood of the Tahoe, the metal of the hood gave way under Jake's weight, helping to cushion his fall. He slid down the side of the now well-dented hood and focused on the exit of the parking garage about 20 to 30 yards away.

As he headed for the exit, Jake took a quick look back to catch a glimpse of his pursuer and saw that Doogan wasn't going to be content with taking the long way around any more. He too was about to vault over the three-foot wall in the same place as Jake. Jake heard the detective as he landed heavily on the hood of the Tahoe. Too bad we don't have time to leave a note, Jake thought to himself as he sprinted for the exit. Two more shots from Doogan's revolver reverberated through the cavernous garage. Both missed Jake, but now another sound caught Jake's ear…the sound of squealing tires echoed throughout the structure. At least one County car was now in pursuit of the news anchor who knew too much.

Jake's opening to the outside world grew ever larger as he continued to sprint toward the exit. It seemed like an eternity, but in seconds Jake was there. Just a small concrete down-slope separated him from the street. Jake took a quick look back and saw that he had actually put a bit more distance between him and the burly detective. Suddenly the sound of a fast moving vehicle could be heard coming down the exit ramp.

Jake turned quickly to make a dash for the street, but he hadn't gone halfway down the short concrete incline when another large white sedan came into view, screeching to a stop in the street outside, directly in front of the exit of the parking garage, blocking Jake's escape.

Jake turned around to see Detective Doogan closing in fast. Right behind the detective Jake saw the headlights of the young deputy's patrol car as it made the turn from the ramp to the bottom level. Jake turned his attention back to the white sedan that had just blocked his only way out. The driver's door swung open hard, and out climbed the mysterious man who had cornered Jake in Rick Rollins' bar. No time now for Jake to tell him that he was certainly right...that he had gotten himself involved in something he shouldn't have. The stranger in the dark suit was moving quickly to make good on his warning. Now standing by the driver's side of the car, the man in the slicked back hair turned to face Jake. A semi-automatic pistol was already in his hand as he used the top of the sedan to steady his aim. Jake instinctively took another look to his rear. There stood Detective Doogan, gasping for air, but slowly raising his own pistol to get Jake in his sites. Funny how at times like these, weird things creep into your mind. Jake suddenly recalled the lyrics to a Stevie Ray Vaughn song, "caught in the crossfire."

Jake turned to face the street again as he heard the first gunshot. He saw the flash from the barrel as the man behind the sedan took dead aim. Jake braced himself for the pain the bullet would bring as it tore through his flesh...but it never came. Instead Jake's attention turned to the noise behind him. Detective Doogan had dropped his revolver. It rattled across the concrete as he clutched his chest. Blood gushed through his fingers. Doogan made an awful gurgling noise and fell face first onto the ground.

Suddenly the man who fired the shots from the street yelled, "Jake get down...flat on the concrete and don't move."

As Jake hit the deck, the sound of running footsteps filled his ears. Up into the garage stormed about a dozen men in combat boots, helmets, and gray fatigues carrying assault rifles. They all wore dark gray bulletproof vests. Emblazoned on each of the vests were three large white letters...FBI.

CHAPTER 26

Flat on his stomach, Jake turned his head to follow the agents in riot gear as they rushed inside the parking garage. Four of the men quickly surrounded the patrol car, and with weapons pointed directly at the driver, the young deputy slowly exited the patrol car, hands raised high. Two more agents entered a door to the far right marked "Stairway"; the rest of the men split into two groups and sprinted up both the exit and entrance ramps that led to the top of the structure.

Jake heard footsteps behind him. As he turned, the man in the dark suit with slicked back hair was standing over him. "You can get up now Jake. I think the danger is over."

"What the..." Jake searched for words...it wasn't that they were hard to find...it was that there were so many of them. Finally Jake just let logic take over. "Here I thought you were one of the bad guys...it turns out you were the cavalry."

The man smiled and held out his hand. "Agent Tom Sauers, FBI."

"I guess 'nice to meet you' would be an understatement." Jake grabbed the agent's outstretched hand and gave it a solid shake. "You already know most of my story. So you won't mind my asking you to just start from the top."

"Sure Jake. No problem. I guess we owe you that much after all you've been through." Agent Sauers loosened his tie and cast a glance inside the parking garage. There was no commotion, which seemed to put the agent at ease. He returned his focus to Jake.

"We've been on this case for a little over a month now. Stumbled onto it actually. Border Patrol busted some Mexicans coming across the border with a vanload full of pot. They gave the border boys some cock and bull story about taking the dope to the Mayor of Butterfield. Border cops thought it sounded so crazy it might be true, so they asked us to check it out. We had an agent complete the run with the info the Mexican mules gave us. Damned if the Mayor himself didn't show up to take possession."

The agent took out a pack of cigarettes from his inside jacket pocket. He shook one out…grabbed a lighter from his pants' pocket and lit it. "Problem was, all we had was the Mayor doing a drug deal, that is until you came along. You put the fear of God in 'em. They were on the phone non-stop trying to figure out what to do with you. A few well-placed wire taps and we had a case. If you hadn't gotten involved we'd have been at this for quite a while. And since I apparently couldn't talk you out of your snooping around in the bar that night, we just decided to let you do what you do best, under our watchful eye of course." Agent Sauers took a deep drag from the cigarette. "You're in for a heck of a commendation from the Government Jake."

"Commendation hell," said Jake. "I've got a heck of a lead story for tomorrow's news."

"I'd say you had an exclusive," said Sauers, "and maybe a couple of good quotes from the FBI." Both men turned their attention to the garage. A host of Federal agents were walking their direction, the city's three top officials in tow, their hands cuffed behind them.

As they approached, Jake couldn't help himself. "Sorry boys. Like I said, never underestimate the power of the press."

Jake watched as the three amigos were escorted out of the parking garage.

"My car's not too far from here," Jake said, "Do you think I could get a lift?"

"Not a problem," replied Agent Sauers. "Guess that's the least I can do."

The two men walked toward the street. The fog was as thick as it had been in quite a while. Jake couldn't wait for the warmth of the large white sedan…and he couldn't wait to get to his jeep…grab his cell phone and give Maddy a call. She'd just love this story.